DARE TO PLAY

Dare Nation Novel #3

NEW YORK TIMES BESTSELLING AUTHOR

Carly Phillips

DARE TO PLAY

He's the bad boy of baseball who's about to lose everything.
She needs a husband to get custody of her teenage sister.
Suddenly a marriage of convenience doesn't look so bad.

Pitcher, Jaxon Prescott has a lot on his plate. Major League Baseball. Reputation as a player. And now? He's on the verge of losing it all. He didn't mean to sleep with his general manager's daughter or get into a brawl that was captured on camera. But his notoriety is a problem and everything he's worked for is at risk.

What's a bad boy to do? Marry his sister's best friend to save his career, even if it's the opposite of everything he wants and believes in.

Macy Walker is the sole guardian of her half-sister until the girl's mother returns and wants her daughter back. In order to win custody, Macy needs to provide stability and marrying someone would do the trick. Luckily for her, her best friend's brother needs a wife.

They're this close to getting exactly what they want — as long as they don't fall in love.

A stand-alone novel

Chapter One

W HAT DID YOU buy for the couple who had everything?

Macy Walker spent over an hour in a luxury department store searching for the perfect wedding gift for Damon Prescott and Evie Wolfe. They'd gotten engaged at the end of Fall and were getting married this Saturday, January seventh, in a small ceremony at his mother's house, unlike his sibling Austin and his fiancée, Quinn, who had a huge Valentine's Day wedding planned at a Miami hotel. There were five Prescott/Dare siblings, two in serious relationships and three to go.

Although to hear each of them tell it, nobody had been looking for permanence. It just happened to find them. Macy wondered who was next up to fall in love.

To say Macy had left the gift to the last minute would be an understatement. Unable to discover anything original for the professional football player and his private investigator fiancée, Macy left the store with an expensive vase, gorgeously wrapped, and headed home to her fifteen-year-old sister of whom she had custody.

As she approached the house, a bright red Mazda Miata she didn't recognize sat in the driveway, top down. If her sister had an older friend over, thinking Macy wouldn't find out, she'd be in trouble. Hannah had a tendency to act out and misbehave, and in many ways, Macy understood. Hannah had a lot of abandonment issues, but she still needed discipline and guidance.

Macy pulled her Jetta around the other car, opened the garage, parked, and exited her vehicle. Letting herself inside, she walked through the laundry room area and into the kitchen, stopping short when she saw who sat with Hannah at the table. Tons of makeup and other items covered the surface, with Sephora bags surrounding them.

Oh, hell. Life was about to get interesting and not in a good way. "Hi," Macy said, making her presence known.

"Macy, look! My mom's back!" Hannah popped up from her chair, a smile the likes of which Macy had never seen on her sister's face, and Macy's stomach twisted painfully.

Hannah was a pretty girl who hadn't learned the concept of *less is more* when it came to makeup. She'd just started to wear it last year, and after their dad died, she'd gone full-out rebellious. Black eye liner and heavy mascara. But there were worse things than too much makeup on her face or the pink stripe in her hair. Macy actually liked the coloring if only Hannah hadn't done it without asking permission, along with a second piercing in her ear. Anything she could do to defy Macy, Hannah tried.

Ever since Lilah walked out when Hannah was ten, she'd grown angrier over time and tried to get away with whatever she could on principle, her bad behavior progressing since their dad died. The last thing Macy needed was Hannah's mother's return to give Hannah false hope that her mother was back to be with her. As far as Macy knew, other than a rare happy-birthday email, Hannah hadn't heard from her mother since she'd left.

Lilah had left her family for someone with more money and who could give her a better lifestyle than Macy's father had been able to. Richard Walker had made a good living as an accountant, and their family hadn't wanted for anything. There had also been inheritance money from her grandparents that had boosted their lifestyle, but it hadn't been enough for Lilah.

"Lilah, this is a surprise," Macy said coolly as she placed her keys in a basket on the counter.

Lilah looked up at Macy, not a shred of embarrassment in her expression. "I've done a lot of soul-searching, and I decided it was time to come home to my baby." She reached across the table and squeezed Hannah's hand, her long, manicured nails obviously freshly done. "And I arrived to find her by herself. Where were you, Macy?"

Oh, she would not question Macy's abilities as a parent. She had no right. "None of your business and Hannah is old enough to be home alone."

"Can Mom stay with us?" Hannah looked at Macy with wide, hopeful eyes, and Macy silently cursed Lilah, whose smug smirk told Macy she'd put her daughter up to asking the question.

Narrowing her gaze, Macy wondered what Lilah's agenda was, because the woman always looked out for number one.

"I don't think that's a good idea. We have a schedule and a routine, and I'd like to keep things as they are." Mostly she didn't want Hannah to get used to having her mother around only for her to take off on her once again. The less time she was exposed to Lilah, the better.

"It's okay, honey, I can stay at the hotel." Lilah sighed dramatically.

Ignoring the guilt Lilah tried to lay on, Macy smiled. "Good. Now that that's settled—"

Hannah pushed back her chair and rose to her feet. "You're such a—"

"Watch it," Macy said before Hannah could finish her sentence. "Don't be rude to me. Now I think we should order dinner." Gritting her teeth, she turned to Lilah. "Would you like to stay?"

She shook her head, and her brunette hair highlighted with blonde swept beneath her cheeks. Lilah rose to her feet and gathered her Chanel tote, which must have cost four thousand dollars easily, and smiled. "I wish I could but I have a date." As she stepped around the table, Macy took in her obviously designer outfit and shoes.

So she was divorced again and hunting. And here playing up to Hannah. Why?

"Come walk me out," Lilah said to Macy, her tone not boding well.

Macy waited for Hannah to say goodbye to her mother, glare at Macy, and storm off to her room before turning to her ex-stepmother. "Okay, cut the sweetness-and-light act. Why are you back? It can't be for Hannah since you haven't bothered with her since you left."

Lilah straightened her shoulders, her attitude turning into the real bitch of a woman beneath the fake nice façade. "Because she's my daughter. When I left, I knew your father would take good care of her when I couldn't–"

"Wouldn't," Macy corrected her.

Lilah pursed her lips. "Listen, she's my child. Her father died, and I needed to wrap up a few things before I could come back for her, but I'm here now."

Bullshit, Macy thought. "Nobody heard from you after Dad passed away. You didn't even come to the funeral or extend condolences. I'm not buying this act. I don't know what your angle is, but I know you have one."

Lilah's cheeks flushed red. "It's no act. I plan to take care of my girl."

"Good luck. I have custody. You signed it over to Dad, and I'm her legal guardian now that he's gone."

"Something a court can easily overturn." Lilah had started for the door, then turned back to face Macy. "It's not like you're doing a decent job parenting. Not only was she alone, she told me she's grounded for no good reason, that you're strict and difficult. She's mine and I plan on getting custody." On that note, Lilah walked out the door without looking back.

Macy's heart pounded inside her chest, fear and concern filling her at the thought of losing the sister she loved and the only family she had left. Macy's mother had died from ovarian cancer when Macy was six, and it had just been her and her dad. True, he'd dated like crazy, hating the idea of being alone, but he'd loved Macy and been a great dad.

Life had been good until the stepmother from hell

arrived when Macy had turned thirteen. Her teenage years had been a nightmare with Lilah picking on her to be perfect, but Macy had managed. And when Lilah had disappeared, Macy was there for Hannah.

At twenty-eight years old, Macy had moved into her own apartment a few years ago, and though she'd helped her father with her half sister, Macy had had a life of her own. But when it became clear her father couldn't handle raising Hannah alone, Macy had moved back into her childhood house, a patio home in a residential neighborhood just north of Miami. With her father gone for eight months now, killed in a car accident, it was just Hannah and Macy.

She'd all but raised her sister, and she had no intention of losing custody to a woman who didn't know how to be a parent.

* * *

ALTHOUGH MACY HADN'T slept well because Lilah's threat to take Hannah stayed with her, she pushed herself to go to Damon and Evie's twilight wedding that evening. She dropped Hannah at a friend's for the night and headed over to Damon's mother's house.

She placed her present on the gift table, picked up a glass of champagne, and because Damon's sister, Brianne, Macy's friend and the connection that had brought her to this party in the first place, was upstairs with the bridesmaids, Macy wandered around by herself. She glanced out the windows, the flowers and white arch for the ceremony a beautiful sight.

When everyone made their way outside, she chose a seat on an aisle, a tissue in her hand because she always cried at weddings. Under a setting sun and in beautiful weather, the bridesmaids wearing pale peach and the groomsmen in tuxedos, Macy sighed with happiness for the couple.

The ceremony was brief but beautiful. As Damon and Evie held hands, whispering vows only they could hear, Macy couldn't help but think she'd never see this kind of love. At her age and with her responsibilities, with no real time to have a social life and working from home, meeting someone interested in a lifetime commitment was almost impossible. And the men she did meet had no patience for her priorities.

She glanced at the groomsmen, her gaze coming back again and again to Jaxon Prescott, Bri's Major League Baseball-player sibling, the word *player* having more than one connotation in his case. Jaxon's reputation for partying and sleeping around was legendary. Of all the Prescott brothers, Austin, the sports agent, Damon, the football player, and Braden, the doctor who she'd only seen in photographs since he was out of the country for Doctors Without Borders, Jaxon was the best looking, at least in Macy's mind. Clean-cut, jet-black hair, chiseled features, full lips she wouldn't mind kissing, and muscles galore, he'd tempt a nun to sin.

He met her gaze, and though she blushed at being caught staring, she didn't look away until he smiled and winked at her, causing her to glance down.

Damn, the man tempted her. He flirted in a way that made her girly parts sit up and take notice. And she was long deprived in that area. But as much as he liked to tease and flirt, she didn't take Jaxon seriously. He was a ladies' man in every sense of the word, and she was the kind of woman who wanted a forever kind of relationship someday. The type that would send Jaxon running at the mere thought of the permanence she desired.

When the vows were complete and the ceremony finished, the bride and groom walked out hand in hand, excited and satisfied smiles on their faces. The bridal party followed, and finally the crowd made their way back inside.

Despite Jaxon standing out, as she looked around at the guests, she couldn't help but be overwhelmed by the sexiness of the men in the room, and the fact that they were dressed up only added to their appeal. Most of them were athletes, and Macy had to admit she'd come up in the world since meeting Brianne Prescott at an exercise class and becoming fast friends.

Finally Bri joined her, snagging a champagne glass off a waitress's passing tray. "Whew, it was hot outside."

"But so beautiful," Macy said of the wedding itself. "And let me tell you, there's a lot of testosterone in this room." She waved a hand in front of her face.

"Eew." Brianne wrinkled her nose in disgust at Macy's comment. "Three of those men in that group you're talking about are my brothers."

"Oh, come on. Besides them. Look around you. You can't deny the hotness."

Brianne, a publicist at Dare Nation, a sports agency owned by her brother Austin and uncle Paul, was used to dealing with professional athletes, while Macy had been taken out of her comfort zone at many of these events. But going to football games and other PR occasions gave her social life a boost she wouldn't otherwise have in between raising Hannah, and for that she was grateful.

She didn't want to spoil Bri's enjoyment of the day by telling her about Lilah's visit yesterday, despite the fact that she couldn't shake the incident or fear of the future from her mind. Losing her sister couldn't happen. It just couldn't.

"Oh, look at the motley crew coming our way," Bri said with a grin on her face. "Evie excluded, of course."

Damon, Evie, and Jaxon strode over, the bride and groom obviously making their rounds, Jaxon tagging along, and as his gaze locked on hers, her stomach did a sensual flip.

"Hi, ladies," Jaxon said, his gaze sliding over her, making her shiver. "You're looking good, Macy. White looks great with your tan. Hot." He treated her to yet another wink, that adorable grin on his face one she couldn't ignore.

Though she was shocked he'd noticed the white halter dress she'd taken an hour to choose, at least that fluttering feeling in her stomach took her mind off her problems.

"Thanks, Jaxon."

"Just telling it like it is. You're blushing." Reaching out, he stroked a finger down her cheek, the calluses on the pads rough, masculine, and making her tingle. "You must not get complimented enough. I could change that."

And crazily enough, under the right circumstances, she might let him. Lord knew she wouldn't be having a relationship of any substance for at least another three years, until Hannah graduated high school and moved out. Did Macy intend to be celibate until then? She shook her head. What the hell was she thinking? Jaxon flirted but he wasn't seriously interested in anything with her.

Just then, Bri slapped her brother's arm. "Leave her alone. So what were you three whispering about?" she asked Damon, Evie, and Jaxon.

"Just asking Jaxon what he's been doing," Damon said.

"You mean *who* he's been doing," Bri muttered, because Jaxon did tend to get into trouble. Months ago, there'd been a viral video with his manager's young – though of age – daughter. Not that he'd known who she was at the time, at least according to Bri, whose job it was to make him look good in the media.

Macy stifled a laugh at her joke, and Jaxon narrowed his gaze at his sister. This was their usual dynamic, Bri calling him out, Jaxon getting not seriously annoyed but letting her know he didn't appreciate the jab.

"Come on, Macy. Let me introduce you to a few people from work. I think you'll like Adam Martsoff," Bri said in an obvious attempt to pull her away from Jaxon.

"He's too boring for her," Jaxon said in what actually sounded like an annoyed tone.

Ignoring him, Bri ushered Macy away from her brother, and Macy told herself she didn't mind. That it couldn't hurt to meet a nice guy who would stop her from thinking about what it would feel like to have

Jaxon's solid body rubbing against hers.

Unfortunately, her hopes were dashed as she spent the next few minutes talking to a pleasant, if boring, like Jaxon had predicted, agent from Dare Nation. She couldn't stop comparing this poor staid guy to the more exciting Jaxon Prescott, but she had no legitimate reason to leave until the sound of yelling from across the room caught her attention and she excused herself to see what was going on.

She approached to see Bri and Jaxon mid-argument, family encircling them from all sides.

"What's wrong?" Damon asked.

"Ask Jaxon." Bri folded her arms across her chest, her glare one she used when in business mode.

A glance at Jaxon showed his face was flushed, and Macy wondered what he'd done wrong.

"Come on, let's go have a talk," Damon said to his sibling but Bri shook her head.

"You're not leaving me out of this. I'm his publicist and he's damn well going to need one," she insisted.

"Why?" Damon asked.

Jaxon opened his mouth to explain, when Bri chimed in first. "He neglected to mention he got into a brawl at a lowbrow bar downtown."

"Dude!" Damon shook his head in disbelief.

"I was backing up a teammate! I didn't start the

damned thing."

"But as usual, someone caught it on video." Bri's frown wasn't one Macy would want to face.

Austin came up beside them. Grabbing Bri's cell, he watched the screen with a wince. "God dammit. Don't you know what behave yourself means?" he asked, and as his brother's agent, he had every right to know the answer.

Still, Macy felt sorry for Jaxon if he'd been backing up a friend as he claimed.

"And to say the video has gone viral is an understatement. I'm getting notifications like crazy." Bri continued to shoot daggers at her bad-boy brother.

"Dammit, Jax, when are you going to get your shit together?" Austin asked.

"Some asshole in the bar was throwing shit at Dale Macaffrey for his missed catch in the playoffs. And he swung first. His friends jumped on and Mac needed reinforcements." Jaxon folded his arms across his chest defensively.

"Come on, guys. You never know where the paparazzi or asshole fans are going to be," Damon said in an attempt to help his brother out.

"My point exactly!" Bri poked her finger at her brother.

"Not *my* point. I was saying cut him some slack. A decent teammate helps out his buddies." Damon tried again to stand up for Jaxon.

Austin groaned. "Regardless, it looks bad, and management is going to be pissed. But we are not doing this here. Not today. Today is Damon and Evie's celebration." Always the head of the family, he took the lead, and his siblings usually listened.

Glancing at Jaxon, he said, "I hope you're prepared for a meeting with ownership, because once they see this video, you're going to be in for it. So will Mac but I don't represent him."

Everyone, including Macy, grimaced at Austin's furious tone, but Jaxon just looked pissed off.

After some more family discussion and murmuring quietly, Damon and Evie said their goodbyes, leaving for their honeymoon to celebrate their happiness, while Jaxon headed for the bar and asked for a drink.

Macy waited until Bri was alone and walked over to her friend. "Hey, are you okay?"

"If I kill my brother, will you bail me out of jail?" she asked, a wry smile on her face.

"If I can afford it, you know I will." Macy laughed. "Is he in that much trouble? Because it sounded like he was just helping out a friend."

Austin joined them. "Doesn't matter. A brawl reflects badly on him."

Bri grasped the drink out of Austin's hand and downed it all in one gulp. "And Jaxon tends to find trouble."

"He needs to mature and settle down," Austin said, as if that were the answer to Jaxon's reputation and problems.

"As if any sane woman would marry him," Bri muttered.

Macy strongly disagreed. "Come on. I know you can't see him this way, but he is easy on the eyes."

Bri made a gagging sound. "I'm going to make some calls," she said and walked away.

Macy kept an eye on Jaxon, who, looking pissed at the world, made his way outside to the patio, where the chairs were still set up, and sat alone on a cushioned chair.

Feeling like he needed company, Macy headed outside to join him.

Chapter Two

J AXON RESENTED BEING humiliated and called out in public even if Bri was his publicist and Austin his agent. Jaxon was a grown man, dammit, and could do whatever he wanted, including backing up a teammate when a jackass made fun of him in public and swung first. His brother had played on a team and damn well knew what it meant to be a stand-up guy. Fucking hypocrite giving him shit now, Jaxon thought.

"Want company?" a familiar female voice asked.

He glanced up. Macy, his sister Bri's friend, had been coming around family gatherings more often lately, and with her understated sensuality, beautiful smile, and charming personality, he'd been intrigued. Flirting came naturally to him, but Macy knew his reputation with women, which was legitimately earned, and he was sure his sister had warned her away from him. She might have blushed a time or two at his compliments, but she hadn't truly engaged with him.

Smart woman.

But that didn't mean the sexual chemistry wasn't there. He felt it and knew she did, too. In fact, he'd caught her watching him when she thought he wasn't looking, like during the ceremony earlier. But he was surprised she'd come out here now.

"Have a seat." He gestured to the free chair next to him.

She lowered herself onto the white folding chair. "Sorry it got ugly in there."

He raised an eyebrow. "You're not here to tell me what a dumb move I made?"

A smile curved her lips. "I kind of admire the fact that you stood up for your friend. Are you really going to get in trouble with management?"

His shoulders stiffened at the thought. He'd given them enough aggravation over the years that they wouldn't be happy no matter the reason. "Probably. Can we talk about something else? Anything else?"

She shrugged. "Sure."

"What's going on with you?" he asked, curious about this woman he'd only seen from afar. This was their first real conversation.

She sighed. "You really don't want to hear my problems."

He tilted his head and glanced at her pretty profile. "Try me."

She shrugged. "Well, I have custody of my fifteen-year-old half sister, and her mother showed up after five years, making noises about wanting custody."

Resting his elbows on his knees, he turned her way. "What happened to your parents, if you don't mind me asking?"

"My mom died when I was six, and Dad passed eight months ago."

Knowing what it was like to lose a parent, even one he hadn't liked that much, because the Prescott family tree was complicated, he grabbed her hand and squeezed it compassionately. "That sucks. I'm sorry."

Her smile was grim. "Thank you."

They sat in silence for a while, the sun beating down on them. Glancing at her from the corner of his eye, he took in her pert nose, those lips he'd imagined kissing, and looking lower, her tanned cleavage, making his mouth water.

"I meant what I said earlier. You look gorgeous in that dress," he said in a gruff voice.

"Thank you." She smiled, her cheeks turning pink in the way they did every time he flirted or complimented her.

It was sweet and endearing. Most women he dealt with were more assured of their sexuality and usually came on to him. He didn't have to work hard for it. There was something captivating about Macy and her air of innocent sensuality.

He glanced down, realizing he still held her hand in his from when she'd told him about losing her parents.

"So I take it you have to get home to your sister?"

To his surprise, she shook her head. "Hannah's sleeping at a friend's tonight."

He hesitated and thought, what the hell? He could feel his siblings' annoyed stare from inside and needed peace. "Want to get out of here? Go somewhere quiet and grab a bite to eat?" he asked, because she was easy to be with and wasn't giving him shit about his life and behavior.

She pulled her bottom lip between her teeth before releasing it. "Are you telling me there are places you can go and not get recognized?"

He shook his head and laughed. "Not really, though some owners and managers are stricter than others about letting people bother their customers. But as you probably know, that doesn't always mean a damn thing. I'd say we could go to my house and order in, but you probably think I'm the big bad wolf," he said wryly.

Her brown eyes met his. "You might be the big bad wolf, but I'm a big girl who can handle you," she said, surprising him.

He rose to his feet and pulled her up with him. "Let's get out of here," he said. "Damon and Evie are gone, and I don't want to deal with the family. Any reason you need to go back inside?"

"I can touch base with Bri tomorrow. I'm good."

"Follow me to my place? I'm about twenty minutes from here."

He watched as she visibly drew a deep breath. "Relax, Macy. It's just dinner."

She grinned. "Says the big bad wolf."

Chuckling, they walked around front to their cars.

* * *

MACY HAD LOST her mind. Somewhere between walking into the Prescott home and sitting down with Jaxon, her brain had retreated and her libido had taken over. Just dinner didn't have to be just dinner and they both knew it.

As she followed Jaxon's black Range Rover in her Volkswagen Jetta, she knew she was out of her depth, but she wasn't turning around or changing her mind. Driving through the luxury neighborhood, she thought she might throw up. And as she pulled into his driveaway, the house the size of a mansion and containing a four-car garage, she figured she'd used up the bulk of her courage getting here. What happened next was all up to her hormones.

After parking, they walked into his house through the garage, where she saw one vintage car, a sports convertible, and an empty spot. Not being a car person, she couldn't recognize each model but had no doubt they were expensive.

"Let's go to the den. We can hang out and I'll order dinner on an app from my phone. How's Chinese food?"

"Love it," she said, ignoring the fact that she was in a fancy dress and high heels. Those she kicked off, leaving them on the floor beside her.

"Anything in particular you want to eat?"

She rolled her shoulders. "I'm not a spicy fan. I love pork dumplings and an egg roll. Anything else I'm good to go."

"I can work with that." He led her to a huge room with — no surprise — a wall-to-wall-size screen and a massive couch with recliners on either end and gestured for her to sit.

He settled in beside her and turned his attention to ordering dinner.

When that was finished, he moved the remote, and she couldn't help but ask, "Is that screen so you can see yourself life-size?"

Chuckling, he faced her, one arm over the back of the sofa. "Yes, I'm that arrogant." He shook his head. "No. It's that I'm a guy and I like big things."

She laughed, enjoying his sense of humor. She also couldn't miss the sexual innuendo in his comment, which led her to wonder about the size of his package beneath the trousers.

Which caused her to squirm in her seat, and she

decided it was time to change the subject. "So tell me. What's it like playing ball in front of a crowd?"

He leaned close, and the smell of his cologne wrapped around her, the scent of musk and man arousing her beyond belief.

"It's a rush like you wouldn't believe. The roar of the people, the cheers, knowing you can give them what they want."

In his eyes, she saw how much he loved the game. "I take it you have to be a little arrogant to play pro? And believe in yourself that much?"

"You do," he admitted.

The food arrived and they ate in the family room, casually, plates on their laps, telling stories and avoiding her problems with her sister and his issues with his siblings. With the world outside his house, she fell under his masculine, seductive spell, the underlying sexual tension never dissipating, and if Macy had second thoughts about coming here on the ride over, they never surfaced again while sharing a meal. Or as they cleaned up together.

And when he turned to her, a predatory gleam in his eye, she knew exactly what he desired and had every intention of giving it to him.

He met her gaze. "You can leave and we can call it a fun night or—"

Before he could finish his sentence, her lips met

his in a sizzling melding of mouths she'd been waiting for all evening. If she was going to do this, there would be no regrets or looking back, and she would enjoy every second in this hot athlete's arms.

He took over without hesitation, backing her against the counter, his hands cupped around her neck, bracing her for the onslaught to come. His tongue slid into her mouth, and she tasted him, her entire body coming alive. Heat rushed through her, and she wrapped her arms around his waist, pulling him close.

His erection, thick and hard, pressed against her belly, and she no longer wondered about the size. She could feel every impressive inch of him. He kissed her again, his lips biting one minute and gliding gently the next. Every nip of his teeth sent spikes of awareness shooting directly to her sex. And when his lips traveled over her cheek and found the sensitive spot on her neck, her long-deprived body reveled in the roughness of his facial stubble against her skin.

He'd already shed his shoes, jacket, and tie when they got home, and she reached for the buttons on his white dress shirt with trembling fingers. His sizzling gaze on hers, he grabbed the sides and ripped open the material, buttons scattering.

"Holy hell, that was hot."

"You haven't seen anything yet," he replied.

Her own dress had a zipper in the back. If she were home alone, she'd be lifting it over her head and doing an unflattering shimmy to get it up and off, but she was going for sexier and more dignified here. But dignity was hard to come by in the face of this man's tanned, overly muscular chest, and she placed her paler hands on his fevered skin.

He let out a groan of appreciation and, without a hitch, reached behind her and unzipped the dress, which immediately fell to the floor.

He took in her matching white silk and lace bra and thong set, bought especially for the dress, tracing the scalloped edge with his rough fingertip. "Now *that* is hot."

Her sex pulsed at his husky tone, the desire he felt for her obvious in his voice, the darkening of his irises, and the taut lines of his face. She swallowed hard, waiting with bated breath because he obviously wanted to be in charge.

He braced his big hands around her waist and lifted her onto the counter, the granite cold beneath her thighs, but she didn't have to wait long to be warmed up. He spread her legs with his hands and stepped between them.

Skin quivering, she looked into his eyes, and the heat and desire she saw there took her breath away. With a flick of his fingers, he'd opened her bra's front clasp. He drew the straps down far enough to confine her arms, dipped his head, pulled her nipple into his mouth, and she saw stars. He devoured first one breast, then the next, arousing her into a frenzy. Moisture coated her thong and desire thrummed inside her.

She glanced down, his black hair in inky contrast with her fair skin, and she wanted him inside her, filling her. To make her point, she shook off the bra and slid her hands between them, undoing the hook on his slacks, and as they dropped to the floor, she curved her finger into his boxer briefs and worked them down his thighs, where they would stay until he chose to push them down the rest of the way.

In the meantime, she curled her hand around his cock, swiping her thumb over the pre-come on the tip, gripping and sliding her hand up and down his straining shaft.

Eyes on his, she lifted her finger to her mouth and sucked on the salty mixture, emboldened by how much he obviously wanted her.

"You're a dirty girl, Macy. Who knew?"

Certainly not her, she thought, bringing her hand back down and continuing to smooth the wetness over him, pumping her hand up and down his cock. A groan shook his big body, and he yanked her toward him, kissing her, tongue thrusting into her mouth and swirling around, making her dizzy.

He took a step back, kicked off his pants and box-er briefs, and removed his socks, only to return and lift her off the counter. She wrapped her legs around his waist, holding on as he walked her upstairs to his bedroom. She barely had time for a glimpse of the shuttered windows surrounding the room and the huge four-poster bed in the center before he lowered her to the mattress, yanked her legs so her body slid to the edge of the bed.

He ripped off the thong and she gasped. As she looked up, a sexy grin lifted his lips. "I need to taste you, too."

And then he lowered himself to his knees, spread her legs, and began to devour her like a starving man. His tongue was talented and never stayed in the same place for too long, licking, nipping, lapping until she didn't know what sensation was coming next, but each one brought her higher. Waves of need teased her but didn't hold on long enough for her to let go and come.

Damn man knew it, too.

"Jaxon, please." She raised her hips and ground into his mouth, unashamed to try and take what she needed.

"When I've had my fill." He slid a finger inside her and began to thrust, taking her off guard.

She'd been empty and needed to be filled, and he'd

sensed that need. One finger became two, and she cried out at the insistent movement. And when he curled the tips in just the right motion, he hit a spot that made her go temporarily blind, and then her body exploded, the orgasm the hottest one she'd ever had, and his cock wasn't inside her yet. She rolled her hips, waves and waves of delicious warm heat rippling through her.

Before she could catch her breath, she heard the rippling of foil from a condom, and then Jaxon poised at the edge of the bed, working his cock into her tightness.

She groaned at his slick fullness. "It's been a while."

A softness she hadn't expected touched his eyes and filled his expression as he slowed, inching into her. Arching her hips, she moaned as she stretched to accommodate him until finally he was completely inside her.

Ripples started to tease her once more. "Move," she said. "I'm good."

"You got it, sweetheart." He spread her knees wide and began to take her hard, slamming into her, only pausing once early on to check that she was okay. Then it was fast and rough, her body feeling his rigid, thick cock tunneling in and out, finding the perfect rhythm.

She'd never had such amazing sex before. No doubt Jaxon Prescott was ruining her for all other men, but at the moment, she didn't care. A second orgasm was brewing, and that was a unique thing for her. She was lucky if she had one during rushed sex before she had to get home to Hannah the few times she'd allowed herself the luxury. Now?

Jaxon's rough fingertip slid over her clit while his incomparable cock hit home. And then she was screaming, again something she'd never done. Not even with her vibrator.

"Oh, shit, I'm coming." But it wasn't enough. She needed more. She needed him. "Harder, Jaxon, please."

He complied, thrusting faster, deeper until her eyes rolled in the back of her head and she came, the vibrations encompassing every muscle in her body. Two more thrusts and he stilled, the rough groan that came from inside him something she'd be remembering for a long time to come.

*   *   *

JAXON STOOD IN the bathroom with the excuse of cleaning up, but the truth was he didn't want Macy to see the effect she'd had on him after something that was usually a simple act of two people getting it on. She'd completely undone him and he was in shock.

But being the consummate playboy, he shook off the uniqueness of the event and headed out of the bathroom, finding Macy fast asleep on top of the covers.

Instead of waking her, he pulled an extra blanket from his closet, covered her, and climbed in beside her. Though he didn't typically bring women back to his house, preferring hotel rooms or their place, where he could make an easy exit, Macy wasn't his normal lay. She was his sister's best friend. He'd be seeing her again, and he needed to end things on a decent note.

Something he'd deal with tomorrow.

He had his reason for keeping all relationships casual, and it was a solid one. He'd had his heart broken before, and he never wanted to experience that pain again.

Katie, his college girlfriend and the woman he thought he'd marry, had taught him a hard lesson. She had dumped him after he'd been traded to Washington in his first deal, not willing to give up her life to be with the man she'd claimed to love. The lifestyle on the road wasn't for her, or so she'd said, despite the fact that she'd known what she was getting into going in. Or maybe it had been that his starting salary wasn't good enough. Who the hell knew.

What he'd learned for sure was that his father, Jesse, had been right. No woman would want him, and Jaxon refused to let that be proven true again. So he'd locked up his emotions and lived life to have fun. Not even being dead eliminated the ghost of Jesse Prescott.

Hell, not even finding out that their uncle Paul had been all the Prescott siblings' sperm donor, making Jesse not their biological dad, had undone the damage he'd caused. One and done was a joke among the Prescott brothers, but Jaxon meant it. No woman would hurt him again.

The next morning, he woke up to the sun shining through the shutters he'd forgotten to close, and as he glanced over, Macy was dressed in that gorgeous, white, curve-hugging dress he'd stripped her out of last night. His cock, already hard with morning wood, perked up even more.

"Oh! You're awake. That makes things easier. I don't have to wake you. Zip me?" she asked, sliding her hair away from her back and over one shoulder and sitting down on the bed.

He blinked in surprise and pushed himself up. "You're leaving?" he asked stupidly.

What had he expected? That she'd stay for breakfast, where they'd rehash all the reasons this couldn't happen again? He didn't know how he was going to bring up the subject as it was. Jaxon didn't come back for seconds. Although as he watched Macy attempt to untangle her sexy hair with her fingers, he thought he could make an exception. Just this once for her.

"Macy—"

"Jaxon—" They spoke at the same time.

"You first," he said, leaning against his headboard.

She treated him to a forced smile. "Listen, this was great and all."

Great? he wondered. How about explosive? Mind-blowing? Anything bigger and better than great.

"I really needed a night for myself," she went on, speaking quickly. "But it can't happen again. And there's no need to tell anyone. Especially Bri. No one needs to know."

He blinked. She was giving him the blow-off speech? In all his years since Katie, he'd done the walking away. He couldn't say he liked how it felt being on the receiving end, but at least Macy had made his life easier.

"Agreed?" she asked, her cheeks pink again, embarrassed and nothing like the seductress he'd seen last night.

He nodded. "Agreed. But at least let me walk you out." His mother had raised him to be a gentleman, and he followed that rule as best he could, depending on the woman and the circumstances.

She nodded.

After climbing out of bed, he pulled on a pair of sweats, his trousers from last night probably still on the floor in the kitchen. *That* thought brought memories of her sucking the come off her finger. His cock jerked and he willed the sucker not to make its presence known.

Entering the kitchen behind her, he saw she'd folded his clothes and placed them on the counter. She'd also found cleaner and had sprayed down the granite surface, the container and paper towels also sitting out.

"I couldn't figure out which was your garbage," she said, face adorably flushed.

"Thank you." He placed a hand on her lower back, and his body buzzed at the contact.

Holy shit, what was it with this woman? He needed to get her out of here immediately. He stepped in front of her and led her to the garage, opening the door and hitting the button on the wall.

They reached the car and she turned to face him. He could see her struggling with some internal thought.

Finally she said, "Last night really was incredible." Leaning over, she pressed her mouth to his, swiping her tongue over his lips, the kiss lasting longer than he thought she'd planned.

Then she ducked her head and climbed into the car, immediately starting the engine, then reversing and driving away as fast as she possibly could.

Chapter Three

T HANK GOD HANNAH wasn't coming home until this afternoon, because Macy needed the time to pull herself together and process last night. She had a huge project she needed to work on today. As a web designer, she made her own hours, but that didn't mean she didn't have deadlines. Whether she'd be able to focus or not was another story.

She barely recognized the woman she'd been with Jaxon. She'd been open and sexual and she'd never be the same again. But she needed to shower, sit down to work, and put it behind her, all of which she did. Then, with a glass of iced tea and her laptop open, she settled in. But instead of being able to design, her mind was full of memories of him pounding into her, giving her pleasure and taking his own, along with the delicious aches and pains in her body that reminded her of every moment with Jaxon Prescott.

She was still staring at a mostly empty screen when Hannah came home from her friend's, dropped off by a parent. She left her overnight bag in the laundry room and walked into the kitchen, where Macy sat, still trying to work.

"Hi. How was your night at Holly's?" Macy asked.

"Fine." Hannah opened the pantry, pulled out a box of cereal, grabbed milk from the fridge, and sat across from Macy as she poured herself a bowl.

Instead of making conversation, Hannah shoved spoonful after spoonful into her mouth, her focus on her cell phone. Instagram was her app of choice, and Macy knew better than to interrupt her every-five-minute check for likes.

After a few minutes of silence, Macy's creative energy kicked in, and she started to work, diving into a new premise she thought her client, a restaurant owner, would love.

"Holy shit! You're Insta-famous!" Hannah said loudly, staring at her screen.

"What are you talking about?" Macy had her own Instagram account and opened the app. "What are you looking at?"

"TNZ says you spent the night at Jaxon Prescott's, the baseball player, and there's a picture of you doing the walk of shame after. I don't know whether to say eew or be impressed," Hannah said, her eyes wide.

Macy searched TNZ and found the photo. She stood by her car in Jaxon's driveway wearing last night's wrinkled dress, her hair a ratty mess, Jaxon in the sweats he'd pulled on to walk her outside. The photographer must have been well hidden, because neither one of them had seen him, or she never would have initiated the kiss that got caught on camera.

Her cheeks flushed and burned as she faced her sister. "I don't know what to say." She'd thought her night would be personal and private. A joke considering everything Jaxon did seemed to be caught on camera. He was the playboy the press loved to watch, and she was caught in the chaos.

Hannah studied her with wide brown eyes. "You barely date. I can't believe you were with a hot jock. Wait until my friends see! I'm going to share it!"

"No!" Macy shook her head. "Please?"

"What's the difference? It's public! Everyone will see it anyway. This is going to get me so many likes," she said, going ahead with her share despite Macy's feelings.

Before she could react, her cell rang. Seeing Bri's name, Macy's stomach churned, and she drew a deep breath before answering. "Hello?"

"You slept with my brother?" Bri's voice carried, and Hannah stared, clearly interested in the fallout.

Macy rose and took the call in the family room. "It just happened. We were talking at the party, he was down from you guys getting on him about the brawl, I ... have some issues I haven't told you about yet, and we left to get dinner. One thing led to another..." She trailed off, figuring enough was enough. Bri had already figured the rest out for herself.

"Yeah, I got that from the photo."

"Jaxon can't even get privacy at his own home?"

Bri let out a long sigh. "You wouldn't believe the lengths the paparazzi will go to. I wouldn't be shocked if one was in a tree to get that shot."

"Well, this is awkward," Macy muttered.

"You're an adult. I'm not judging you. I just wish Jax would learn some discretion. Even he knows anywhere outside isn't safe."

"I guess he wasn't thinking?" Before Bri could jump on that comment, Macy went on. "Is this going to get him in more trouble?"

Bri said something to someone and then replied, "Sorry. I was talking to Austin. I don't know. He just doesn't know the meaning of lying low."

"It seems to me a lot of these incidents aren't his fault."

"But they call attention to him anyway. He's got a list a mile long. And listen to you, all #TeamJaxon," Bri said, laughing.

At least she wasn't pissed at Macy. And she hoped Bri wasn't angry at Jaxon, either.

"Listen, I have another call. Talk later." Bri disconnected, and Macy returned to the kitchen to find Hannah talking on the phone.

"Yeah, isn't it cool? *The* Jaxon Prescott, pitcher for the Miami Eagles," she said.

"Who are you talking to?"

"Mom," Hannah said and turned away to continue chatting.

Macy winced and lowered herself into a chair. Hannah had no idea her mother had threatened to go after custody, but if she was serious, Macy had just given her a very wide opening to take Hannah away from her. The last thing she needed was to be portrayed as a groupie or a slut who indulged in one-night stands, getting rid of her sister so she could have sex.

She groaned, putting her head on her arms, wondering what she was going to do now.

* * *

WHEN A MAN couldn't even kiss a woman in the privacy of his own driveway, something was really wrong with the world in general. Fucking paps. Social media. People who lived to see what famous people did in their spare time. They all needed to get a life of their own and stop fucking up his. This time they'd captured a nice girl in their clutches, and that pissed Jaxon off even more. Macy hadn't signed up for his kind of life. Not the way the groupies who followed him from game to game and bar to bar did.

He didn't have a chance to check on her, and even

if he had the time, he didn't have her number, which meant he was going to have to beg his sister to share it. That was the only good thing about him being summoned to Dare Nation.

He walked into the building and headed straight for Austin's office, smiling at the main receptionist on his way to his brother's corner office, where Quinn, Austin's personal assistant and wife, had a desk right outside.

"Hi, Jaxon," Quinn said, greeting Jaxon not with her usual happy smile but a pitying grimace.

"I take it they're waiting for me?" he asked.

She nodded.

"How's my adorable niece?" he asked about the baby, not only because he cared but because the longer he avoided the firing squad inside that office, the better. His brother Austin had found baby Jenny on his doorstep, moved Quinn in to help him navigate being a dad, and the two had fallen in love. Despite Jaxon's cynicism on the subject of love, he was happy for his sibling.

Eyes lighting up at the topic, Quinn went on to tell him all the things the six-month-old baby was learning to do. "And she stands up and bounces on her chubby little legs and she's scooting backwards. Pretty soon she'll be crawling!"

"Said like a proud mama." Jaxon folded his arms

across his chest and grinned. His brother was a lucky man—if Jaxon were to consider settling down with a wife and a baby lucky. Which he most certainly did not.

"Jaxon, stop stalling and get your ass in here!" Austin bellowed from the open door behind Quinn.

Quinn winced. "Guess you better move it."

"It's times like these when it sucks to have family as your agent and publicist."

Quinn's laughter followed him as he headed around her and through the door to face his siblings.

Austin stood behind his desk, arms folded, eyes narrowed, wearing a suit that demanded respect. Beside him, leaning against the floor-to-ceiling dark mahogany bookshelf, waited Bri. High-heeled foot tapping, lips pursed, and also dressed up in her finest suit, she met his gaze.

"Okay, let's have it." Jaxon didn't mean to sound glib but realized, based on his brother's and sister's expressions, that's exactly how his statement had come out.

"Despite the fact that we discussed this at the party, let's start with the obvious. What part of lie low do you not understand?" Austin asked.

"Oh, excuse me. Walking out onto my own driveway is a crime now," he said, well and truly pissed off.

Austin closed his eyes and groaned. "You're right.

It's not your fault, but that doesn't change the fact that you're a staple online, in the papers, and everywhere else. Not to mention you've now made Macy a target for unsavory gossip."

Jaxon winced at that because it was true. Online celebrity sites had jumped all over the photos and were more interested in finding out who the woman he'd been with was, which put Macy directly in the spotlight. Something she probably didn't need or want.

"Sit," Bri said, glancing between her brothers.

Not wanting to piss his sister off further, Jaxon sat.

Leaning back against the sofa, he glanced at his brother and braced himself for whatever came next, but Austin had obviously calmed down. He walked over to the seat beside him and lowered himself onto the cushion, placing one arm on the back of the sofa.

"As your brother, I understand who you are and why you act the way you do." Austin was fully aware of Jaxon's past with Katie and always coming in behind both Austin and Damon because of his choice to play baseball, not football, and disappointing their father.

"But dammit, Jax, you have to grow up." He held up a hand. "I'm not talking about getting caught on your driveway but brawling? You're twenty-eight. Old enough to understand you're nearing the end of your pitching career."

Jaxon's heart squeezed in his chest. "Ouch."

His sibling was hitting on every insecurity he had about his past, old relationships, his job, his career, and his future. The things he partied and drank to avoid dwelling on.

He knew why he'd fallen into this lifestyle, and it wasn't just the woman who'd walked out on him.

Though Jaxon had been fifteen when his father died, Jesse Prescott had been around long enough to have an impact. His asshole father had let him know in no uncertain terms, if he didn't play football, he was useless and no woman would want him. After losing Katie, Jaxon had gone about proving his deceased old man wrong by letting any cleat chaser available into his bed.

Austin didn't flinch at Jaxon's reaction. "It's my job to tell you the hard facts. I know you're in the off-season, but if you want to retire in disgrace, you're well on your way, because if the Eagles want you gone, no team is going to want to pay what's left on your contract, and they're not going to trade for a twenty-eight-year-old with Tommy John surgery two years ago. The reality is you're too old for the partying and sex-with-groupies shit, too."

"Hey! Macy isn't a groupie!" Bri said, taking the words out of Jaxon's mouth before he could say the same thing.

"You know what I mean," Austin said. "Actually, this is worse, because Macy is a nice girl who probably didn't expect her life to be turned upside down by sleeping with you."

Jaxon dipped his head. "Yeah. Linc said the same thing," he admitted, speaking of his best friend, his catcher, and a happily married family man who planned to retire at the end of next year when his contract expired.

Bri strode over and put a hand on his shoulder, offering sympathy. "I represent Linc, too, as you know. He gives me no trouble, he goes to work, does his job, and knows how to stay off ownership's radar. Can't you be more like Linc?"

Jaxon's eyes opened wide. "You mean you want me to get married and settle down? Hell no. No female wants to live the kind of life a baseball player does. I'm constantly on the road and play one hundred and sixty-two games a year, excluding postseason. Not to mention the fact that I was once in a relationship, came damn close to having that married life, and learned it's not in the cards."

Austin groaned. "It *is* possible to live that life with the right woman. Look at Linc."

"You two sound like parrots," Jaxon muttered.

Austin went on. "You won't be playing ball forever. You'll be more settled. And you don't want to be alone for the rest of your life."

"Says the man who not three months ago was a die-hard bachelor. Ever heard the expression the pot calling the kettle black?"

A muscle ticked in Austin's temple. "One, I didn't have to answer to anyone but myself. I was retired. And two, you might learn from my experience instead of being an asshole. Quinn is the best thing that ever happened to me. You should try dating a nice girl and not going for the ones who spread their legs for anyone with a jersey."

"Eww." Bri shuddered. "This isn't a locker room."

"Well, he needs to hear it," Austin muttered. "Macy's a great woman. We all like her. She's the kind of female a guy should settle down with."

"I'm not going to argue about that. She's amazing. But I'm not getting married. And ownership can't make me," he muttered.

Austin shook his head. "No, but they can order you to chill the fuck out or be suspended or, worst case, cut. Is that what you want?"

Jaxon held up his hands in defeat, slamming them on both thighs. "Fine. I'll behave, okay? I'll focus on playing ball when the season starts." Not that he'd ever screwed up a game, but no one seemed to care about his stellar record.

Pushing himself up, he was about to storm out

when Bri called his name. "Jaxon."

She grabbed his arm. "Come with me." She shot Austin a warning look, which Jaxon interpreted as *stay put*. Which was fine with him. He didn't need any more lecturing from his *agent*.

* * *

JAXON FOLLOWED HIS sister to her office, which had a wholly different look from Austin's masculine dark wood shelving and décor. Her walls were painted a turquoise color, her shelves were white, and she had gorgeous pops of color everywhere, from the paintings on the wall to the knickknacks on her desk. Thanks to the scenery, he immediately felt more relaxed.

"Have a seat," Bri said. "Can I get you a soda? Water?"

He shook his head, studying his sister before finally speaking. "What are you thinking?" he asked his brilliant fixer sister.

"I think we need time to pass where you behave like the player your teammates look up to and management doesn't have to worry about seeing in the paper." She waved her hands in the air as she spoke. "They've had it with the bad press. As for me, I'll work on getting you some positive media, and you will lie low. Agreed?"

He nodded. "Agreed." Because despite what it

looked like to the outside world, his career meant everything to him.

Acting out had been his way of defying the father who never respected his determination to pitch and become a Major League Baseball player. To Jesse Prescott, the only acceptable sport was football, a man's sport. And because Jesse had lost his ability to even be drafted in the NFL due to an injury, he'd made damned sure his sons were going to fulfill his dreams.

He'd failed with two of the four. While Austin and Damon went on to play football, Braden had become a doctor, and Jaxon stuck with baseball, his passion, both disappointing their father.

But as they'd discovered last year when their uncle Paul had needed a liver transplant, Paul was the Prescott siblings' biological father. Not Jesse, who had been unable to have children. Another failure. Another reason he'd been so hard on the kids.

If Paul and his mother had fessed up earlier, they might have spared the children Jesse's temper and disdain, but his mom believed she could be a buffer, and neither wanted to make Jesse face his failings. Plus Paul had promised his silence. But with Jesse gone for thirteen years now, there'd been no harm in the revelation, and Austin's kidney had saved Paul's life.

All's well that ends well, Jaxon thought, before

shaking his head to clear the memories and meeting his sister's gaze.

"Are we going to talk about Macy?" Bri asked.

"I'd rather not." His private life was just that.

He didn't screw around and talk about the women in his bed, but in this case, there was more to his reticence. As much as he hated to admit it, he hadn't been able to get Macy out of his head. She'd been different. And he didn't want to think about why.

"Well, tough." She sat down beside him. "She's my closest friend, and there's no way I'm going to let you hurt her."

He frowned. "Thanks for the vote of confidence," he muttered. "Macy and I had an understanding. It was one night." And if anything, she'd been more eager to run than he'd been to have her leave. Something else he had a hard time comprehending.

"It's just not like her. I can't remember the last time she even went on a date," Bri said.

Something Jaxon knew, because even now he could remember how tight she was when he'd thrust into her, how slowly he'd had to work his way inside her. Holding back a groan, he met his sister's gaze. "She mentioned it had been a while."

"Guys don't like the fact that she has responsibilities. She needs to put her sister first and they resent it. In other words, most men are jackasses."

Jaxon chuckled, unable to argue that point. "She told me that her sister's mother showed up out of the blue. She was making noises about wanting custody."

Bri's eyes opened wide. "You're kidding! She didn't say anything to me about that."

"She probably knew you had a lot on your plate with the wedding. I'm sure she'll tell you."

Bri bit her bottom lip. "If that's true, that photograph of you two kissing is going to cause trouble for her, too. It looks bad, her leaving your house the morning after."

Leave it to the PR person to look at the bright side, he thought wryly. "I don't want Macy to have trouble because of me."

"Wishes can't change facts." Bri tapped her foot against the carpeted floor. "I'll call her."

"How about you give me her number and let me handle the problem I caused?" He'd been planning to ask for her number anyway, and knowing his sister's penchant to involve herself in other people's problems, the need to mend issues strong, he needed to take charge of his own life.

With a frown, Bri nodded. "Fine." She picked up her phone and sent over Macy's contact to Jaxon's cell.

It was time he stepped up to the plate and saw if he had, in fact, caused trouble for Macy and, if so, what he could do to fix it.

*   *   *

IT HADN'T TAKEN long for Macy to be recognized while out in public doing errands. People stared and someone even asked her if Jaxon Prescott was as good in bed as he looked. She didn't like the infamy and resented the intrusion into her life. She didn't understand how professional athletes, actors, actresses, and other famous people handled it on a larger scale. But she survived the week and even finished her project on time, making the money she was counting on.

Mostly she managed by staying inside after the first time she was recognized, and though Jaxon had called to check on her, she'd missed his call. He'd left his private number, so she texted him back and lied that she was fine. He didn't need to know how freaked out she was. In another day or two, things would blow over, or so she hoped.

The Friday after her night with Jaxon, Macy braved the great outdoors. She ran a bunch of errands including food shopping and stopping at the pharmacy and dry cleaner, and with her hair pulled back, a hat on her head, and dark sunglasses, nobody bothered her.

She came home and had just finished unpacking everything when the doorbell rang.

She walked over, glanced out, and saw a well-dressed man with a manila envelope in his hand.

Without thinking, she opened the door.

"Macy Walker?" he asked.

"Yes. Can I help you?"

He handed her a large envelope. "You've been served," he said and immediately turned and walked away.

Her stomach jerked as she stepped back and slammed the door at his retreating form. With shaking hands, she opened the seal, although she knew exactly what she'd find.

"I can't believe she did it." Tears of frustration and fear welled in Macy's eyes.

She slammed the letter down on the nearest counter. Now she needed to hire a lawyer she couldn't afford to fight for custody unless she wanted to dip into the insurance money her father had left in trust, and that she didn't want to do. She was smart enough to understand the value of savings. Hannah's share would pay for her college, and Macy wanted backup in case either of them needed it.

She put away the food and cleaning she'd picked up, straightened up the house, and she still couldn't get rid of the feeling of panic. She was too worked up for designing, and her exercise classes were in the evenings, so she put on a meditation app and searched for calm.

Thirty minutes later, she'd found a modicum of relaxation and decided to shower. Once she came out, she checked her phone, surprised to see a call from Jaxon, and her stomach twisted with, dare she admit it, excitement? Despite the infamy, she liked the man, dammit.

When she tapped the play button, the rough sound of his voice caused tremors of awareness throughout her body.

"Hi, Macy. I'm calling to check on you again. Call me back this time."

She stood in the bathroom, towel wrapped around her body, Jaxon's cell number just waiting for her to use. Before she could chicken out, she dialed his private number.

"Hi," she said, trying not to sound breathless, husky, or any other sexy adjective she could think of. Just returning the call of a friend, not the man she'd slept with.

"Hey. How are you?" he asked.

"Oh, just the center of attention everywhere I go," she joked. Sort of. Today had been an easy day recognition-wise.

Of course, his groan sounded sexy. "Shit. I'm sorry. I hope it's just a nuisance? Because it'll blow over."

She stared down at her nails and decided to tell him. "I don't think so. I was served with custody papers today. Apparently I'm an unfit guardian."

"Dammit." He paused and the silence grew between them.

"It's not your fault," she said, knowing from Bri he'd been read the riot act by Austin, even though they all agreed he hadn't done anything wrong being in his own driveway. It was the accumulation of issues that was Jaxon's problem.

"I can't help feeling responsible. How about we meet at an out-of-the-way place and talk?" he asked.

She glanced down at the towel and then in the mirror at her wet hair. "I need about an hour," she said, figuring that included travel time. "Text me where and I'll see you there."

"Sounds good. And Macy?"

"Yes?"

"I'm sorry to drag you into my mess."

She smiled at that. "As I recall, I went willingly."

He was laughing as he ended the call.

Chapter Four

J AXON WAITED FOR Macy at Central Ave., a bar and
grill he frequented but one that was dark, with a
bartender who'd kick anyone's ass if they bothered a
customer. Famous or otherwise.

"Hey, Beckett. I'll have a Bud Light." Jaxon spoke
to the owner and bartender he'd known for years.

"You got it." Beckett reached for a beer and
popped the top, sliding the bottle across the counter.

"How's it going?" he asked.

"You already know, don't you? You watch TNZ
along with the rest of America." That photo of him
and Macy hadn't just gone viral, every entertainment,
social media, and television show had picked it up,
probably because she was a fresh face and someone to
speculate about.

"True but it's my job to get you talking," said the
man who was as much a friend as a bartender.

About a decade older than Jaxon, Beckett Halstead
had inherited the bar from his father and knew every
customer who came through the door.

Jaxon didn't want to go through a woe-is-me story.

He'd already dragged a good person down with him. Hearing that Macy had a serious custody issue on her hands had him feeling extra guilty. He had no doubt that photo had provided the ammunition her stepmother needed to go ahead with her threat. "I really don't feel like talking."

Beckett nodded as he wiped down the bar with a rag. "Okay, well, just know this. As soon as the next big story hits, you'll be yesterday's news. You just need to ride it out."

If only it were that simple.

Jaxon scrolled through the social media on his phone, getting lost in other people's curated lives, when he sensed someone slide into the chair beside him, looking exhausted. No less pretty but pale, tired, and wiped out.

"Can I buy you a drink?" he asked.

She shook her head. "I'm just going to eat a quiet meal, head back home, and crash until Hannah gets home from school." She let out a tired sigh that sounded exactly like how he felt.

"Well, you need to have something." He gestured to Beckett. "Get the lady a…"

"Club soda," she said. "I really can't drink. The last thing I need is to have a problem driving home or for my sister to smell alcohol on my breath."

"Club soda and your lunch on me," Jaxon confirmed with the bartender.

She propped an arm on the bar. "Is this you being charming?" She swung her legs around to his side of the stool, turning toward him.

He grinned. "It's me being a friend." It was his way of reaffirming their status.

Beckett slid her glass across the bar and she took a sip. "So we're friends now?" An amused grin lifted the corners of her mouth. A mouth he wanted to kiss again.

"I think we qualify." He lifted his bottle and touched her glass. "To friends."

"To friends."

Friends who'd made out on his kitchen counter and had the hottest sex of his life in his bed. He shifted in his seat, his cock stiff at the memories.

He stared at the bottle in his hand, letting the condensation cool him off.

"So what's got you down today? I know Bri said Austin gave you a hard time."

He nodded. "I also had a call with my manager. That brawl isn't going to be forgotten any time soon. I hate disappointing my team, management, and my family," he admitted.

"I'm sorry." She wrinkled her nose as if in thought. "If it's any consolation, everything passes in time."

Same thing Beckett had said, and he appreciated

her attempt at making him feel better. "But in the meantime, things suck. And Austin's solution was to tell me to settle down and get married." He let out a half laugh, still certain that was the worst idea he'd ever heard.

She grinned. "Not ready to give up the bachelor lifestyle?" Her half smile made him chuckle.

"Not in this lifetime."

She swirled the ice in her glass with the straw. "You know, getting married would help me, too. Hannah's mother has got a lot of strikes against her, but she's still her biological parent, while my current reputation has me branded as a groupie. But if I could offer her a stable home with two parents, the judge would look at me a lot more favorably." She took a sip of her drink, eyeing him over the top of the glass.

"Jesus. I am so sorry for causing you problems," he said, well aware she wasn't teasing nor was she hinting.

She shrugged. "It's not your fault paparazzi follow you around. It just sucks for both of us."

He didn't sense any guile. Just an honest statement in response to his mention of marriage as a solution. But the wheels in his brain began to turn.

"No prospective male friend in your life willing to step up?" he asked, unsure if he wanted her to say yes or no.

"Nope." Her shoulders dropped dejectedly.

He studied her delicate profile, and something twisted in his chest as he felt a shift inside him. Not that he wanted to get married. He didn't. He valued his independence and the life he lived, but the fact was that he'd helped cause her dilemma with Hannah. True, her stepmother had been making custody threats before they'd been caught making out on his driveway, but she certainly looked a lot less parental thanks to him.

And there were even more reasons the action made sense. She stood to lose custody of her sister. He stood to lose, well, everything. Austin had made it clear his lifestyle and behavior jeopardized how he went out at the end of his career. And he'd worked too damned hard to get where he was in the majors to blow it over juvenile stupidity now.

Marriage to Macy was a radical, crazy idea. They didn't know each other well, but they sure as hell were sexually compatible. More than any woman he'd been with before.

He took a sip of his beer. "If there *were* a willing man, would you consider getting married?" he asked, wondering where she stood on the matter.

She paused from drinking her soda and met his gaze. "I don't know. I never had a reason to give it a thought." She visibly swallowed hard. "Why are you asking?"

Was it hope he saw in her beautiful brown eyes?

A mixture of panic along with a sort of resolution rose up in his throat. "I don't know why I'm asking, really. There's a part of me that thinks we could solve each other's problems and another part of me that wants to hurl at the very idea," he said honestly.

She burst out laughing. "You've got to be kidding. Bad boy Jaxon Prescott is considering getting married?"

"I wasn't." Until he'd spoken to her. He curled his fingers tighter around the bottle.

"Yeah. Not in this lifetime is what I believe you just said."

He glanced at her, really considering. They needed the same thing. A settled, family appearance. A way for her to keep her sister and for him to calm his team management so he didn't end his career in humiliation. But such a sudden notion had him feeling queasy after he'd been refusing his brother's mere mention of the idea.

Still, there was something about the notion he couldn't dismiss. "Your problems are as big if not bigger than mine. You're Bri's friend, a good person, and the more I let it sink in, I think marriage could help us both." His pulse jumped and his heart rate sped up as he began to more seriously consider it.

"Jaxon—"

"Why don't we order and we can talk?"

She stared at him, her mouth open. "You're serious?"

He nodded.

As if in slow motion, she picked up a bar menu, took a look, and gestured for Beckett. "A plain burger and fries. Medium well, please."

Jaxon grinned. "So we have the same taste in food. One more thing in common." He didn't mention their compatibility in bed. That was a given.

He glanced at the bartender. "I'll have the same thing."

Beckett walked over to the pass-through to the kitchen and called in the order before getting back to work doing inventory behind the bar.

To ease the tension with Macy, Jaxon began talking about his upcoming season and recent trades to his team, sidestepping their problems and his marriage idea for the moment. But the longer he sat making easy conversation, the more he realized he could be with Macy and not feel suffocated. A fifteen-year-old girl in his house? That he wasn't so sure about, but her half sister would be part of the deal.

"What do you do for a living? When you're not corralling a teenager, that is?" he asked.

"Web and graphic design. When Hannah, that's

my sister, when her mother left her with my dad, I knew I needed to go to a local college and find a job I could do from home so I could help him out. Hannah and I have a thirteen-year age difference," she explained. "Dad needed me and so did she."

"Food, folks." Beckett slid their plates in front of them.

"Thanks," they both said at the same time.

Jaxon wasn't surprised that Macy was a good daughter, the kind who stepped up when needed.

They finished their meals and he'd run out of time. It was do-or-die time, and he had to trust his instincts on what he was about to ask the woman beside him. "Macy?"

"Yes?" she asked easily, as if she'd either forgotten he'd mentioned marriage or thought he'd dismissed the idea.

"Marry me and solve both of our problems."

* * *

MACY CHOKED ON her club soda, the bubbles going up her nose and down her throat. "I'm sorry. I thought you said *marry me*."

She hadn't meant for him to take her mention of how marriage would help her custody situation as a hint. And after a little while, he'd stopped questioning her about it and they'd gone on to talk about normal things. Now he wanted her to marry him?

He patted her on the back, waiting until the tears stopped and she dabbed at her eyes with a napkin.

"You're not serious," she said when she could finally speak.

"While we were talking, I was sorting through the idea in my mind, and the hard truth is that we both need this. For one thing, my agent and publicist would love the idea."

"That same publicist will think I've lost my mind," she said of her best friend.

He grinned, showing an adorably sexy dimple. "She'll come around. Everyone in the front office at the Eagles is going to be thrilled. And in return, it will help repair your reputation. I know I'd feel better helping to fix what I caused. And I'll be there for you in court, and we'll put up a united front. I'm telling you, this is a win-win."

It sounded like insanity to her. Insanity that just might gain her the end result she wanted. Custody of Hannah. "Can I give it some thought? I mean go home, let the idea settle?"

"Of course."

Beckett placed the check in front of him, he paid, and they walked to her car in silence. She assumed he was as lost in thought as she was, considering this insane idea.

He stopped at her door.

She was alone with the handsome athlete she hadn't been able to get out of her mind since last weekend. She'd replayed every moment in his house from beginning to end, orgasm to orgasm, and she'd be lying if she said her stomach wasn't twisting with awareness again now.

Especially with the prospect of marriage between them. She looked up, meeting his expectant gaze.

"Seriously give the idea some thought, okay?" he asked in a rough, sexy voice. "Forget about me, I want to make this right for you."

She nodded. "I promise, I will." She wouldn't be able to think of anything else, and she couldn't deny she appreciated the fact that he was taking responsibility for her current situation with Lilah.

He reached for the door handle, his head close to hers. Without warning, he straightened and backed her against the warm metal of the car, his face and lips close to hers.

"What are you doing?" she whispered.

"Reminding you of our compatibility," he said, brushing his lips over hers and lingering there.

The move stunned her, but the second he kissed her, she melted like butter in the hot sun. Her lips parted and he slid his tongue inside. Electricity arced between them and her body came alive. The spark of chemistry between them exploded like it had last weekend, and she wanted nothing more than to plaster herself against him, but before she could do more than think, he pulled back.

"We don't want to get caught again. Unless we can say we're engaged. Then any photo is a good photo. But I made my point," he said, a pleased grin on his face.

"And what was that?"

He tweaked a long strand of her hair. "If we are going to get married, we're not going to be celibate."

She blinked. "Whoa. Slow your roll, Mr. Playboy. I didn't even agree to marry you yet, let alone have it be a real marriage." She stared at him, surprised by the understanding expression on his face.

"You have a lot to think about. And so do I."

"Considering changing your mind already?" she asked him, surprised by how panicked she was at the notion.

Maybe she wanted this fake marriage more than she'd thought. Which was another thing for her to consider. He was the playboy; she was the kind of woman who could fall hard and fast. And that scared her more than the proposal she was considering.

* * *

AS MACY DROVE home, her entire body was aware of

Jaxon's kiss and proposal. Having already experienced the magic of Jaxon Prescott in bed, she had to ask herself if she could handle living with him, sleeping with him, and not getting her heart broken in the process when their union came to an end.

Because Jaxon didn't want to be tied down and she didn't do casual sex. Her night with him had been an aberration, one she'd needed, but it wasn't her MO. To Macy, sex meant something or would come to. This marriage would have an expiration date, and she didn't trust herself to sleep with him and not end up with her heart engaged. But she couldn't deny that they both needed the results this union could provide.

She pulled into the driveway, surprised to see Lilah's car, and her stomach churned with dread. Though she'd allowed Lilah to pick Hannah up, school had just ended, and they'd barely had time to get home. Wondering why they weren't out shopping as planned, Macy headed inside, but Hannah and her mother weren't in the kitchen, the family room, or anywhere she'd expect them to be downstairs.

As she walked toward Hannah's room, she heard their voices, giggling and happy. It wasn't that she didn't want Hannah to have a relationship with her mother if Lilah could step up as a parent, but she didn't want Hannah to be happier being with her mother than with Macy. And from the peals of laughter Macy hadn't heard from Hannah in a while, that was exactly how her sister was feeling.

She stepped into the doorway and immediately saw the suitcase open on Hannah's bed, Lilah sitting beside the luggage. Hannah must have been in the bathroom in the hall.

Worried, she cleared her throat. "Hi."

"Well, well, well, isn't it the star of social media? Or should I say social media slut?" Lilah batted her eyelashes not so innocently.

Macy narrowed her gaze. "You don't know what you're talking about."

"But a judge might."

Hannah came bouncing past Macy into the room. "Macy! Mom said I could sleep over tonight. She's staying at the Nobu Hotel on Miami Beach. Oh! I need my toothbrush!" she cried and ran for the bathroom off her bedroom, pushing Macy aside.

Looking pleased, Lilah grinned at Macy before focusing on her iPhone.

Macy's stomach twisted, both at Lilah's accusation and at the confrontation to come, because as she looked at Hannah, she saw the loaded cosmetic bag in hand. It looked like she was going for a lot more than one night.

"Hannah, you didn't ask me if you could go, and you know you're grounded this weekend."

Her sister stilled. "I assumed me being with my mother was different than going out with friends."

"Maybe it would have been if you'd asked permission." God, was she always going to come out as the bitch when it came to dealing with Lilah?

"You can't stop me from sleeping at my mother's."

Lilah, of course, stayed out of it, not without a smirk, of course, knowing it was better for Macy and Hannah to argue to drive a deeper wedge between them.

Macy glanced at her sister. "Please don't leave. I'll be back to talk more in a few minutes."

She needed to think strategically. What was best for Hannah? What looked best to the court especially now that her own reputation had taken a hit? God, she needed a lawyer.

Unsure of who to call but knowing she needed to bounce the ideas circling her head by someone, she pulled out her phone, and after she unlocked her screen, Jaxon's number stared back at her.

He wasn't her friend, not really, but he was the person who'd offered to insert himself in her life and help her sort out her issues. She wondered if he really meant it, and as she tapped his name, she knew she was about to find out.

She listened as the phone rang, surprised when he picked up almost immediately.

"Macy?"

"Hi." She bit down on her lower lip. "If you were serious about our situation, I could use some backup right now. And afterwards we can discuss my answer to your proposition."

"Just tell me where to go. I'll be right there," he said without hesitation.

She gave him her address and hoped he could help her make the right decision tonight for her future.

Chapter Five

C ALL HIM INTRIGUED. Since Jaxon had just seen
Macy a short time ago, he wondered what had
her reaching out to him so quickly.

He pulled into the driveaway of the modest house,
a little smaller than the one he and his siblings had
grown up in, and cut the engine of his Range Rover. A
red sport convertible sat in the driveaway, which he
doubted belonged to Macy. He'd walked her to a Jetta
earlier, and she didn't seem the type to have a sports
car on the side.

Since leaving her, his heart had been racing and his
anxiety high as he wondered what his future held. On
the one hand, he was petrified of losing his bachelor-
hood and lifestyle, and he had to keep reminding
himself that their arrangement wouldn't be permanent.
Besides, there was a lot to like about Macy, which
calmed some of his fears. She was easy to be around,
low-maintenance, and she knew going into the marriage that he'd be on the road often once the season
started.

The one thing he didn't worry about was sexual

chemistry. They had it in spades. Now he just had to convince her to make their marriage a real one. He wasn't kidding when he said he didn't plan on being celibate. And he wasn't a cheater, which meant they were going to have to agree on a true marriage.

He parked the SUV, climbed out, locked the door, and walked up the path leading to the front door, passing the well-kept foliage along the way. He rang the bell and waited, hands in his front jeans pockets.

Macy opened the door, looking worried, and he had the sudden urge to pull her into his arms and reassure her everything was going to be okay. "What's going on?"

"Come in," she said, stepping aside so he could enter the house.

He walked into the foyer with white and light pink faux texture on the walls and a pretty landscape of photographs hanging in the hall.

She stepped closer, the scent of her floral perfume a reminder of how hot she was in bed.

"Thank you for coming." She spoke softly.

"What's wrong?"

She drew a deep breath. "My former stepmother is upstairs, and she's planning to take my sister, Hannah, with her to her hotel. Hannah said it's for the night, but she's packing as if it's for much longer. She's a rebellious teenager. If I forbid it, I'm going to alienate her even more. If I allow it, I risk not being able to get her back, and it doesn't help that Lilah brought up our one-night stand and the social media attention it got." She appeared pale and shaken.

"What's your gut telling you?" he asked.

"That I need to see a lawyer."

He nodded. "I agree. But in the meantime?"

She sighed. "I'm inclined to let her go. Act as reasonable as I can but insist she come home tomorrow, and give Lilah a chance to prove she's not fit to be a mother or, better yet, let her get bored of the responsibility."

He grasped her hands in his. "Then trust yourself. Now another question. Why did you call me?"

A wry smile pulled at her lips. "Because I need backup from *my fiancé* to make sure my ex-stepmother from hell understands she has to bring Hannah back tomorrow. *Or else.*"

His heart pounded harder in his chest. So this was a go.

"Once Lilah realizes that I got caught leaving my fiancé's house and not some random hookup, she'll realize who you are and the resources at your disposal and think twice about trying to walk all over me." Macy straightened her shoulders. "Not that I'd let her, but I'll take all the leverage I can get. And you, Mr. Famous Baseball Player, give me power I wouldn't otherwise have."

He looked at her, her porcelain skin and pink lips surrounded by gorgeous light brown hair, staring at him with hope and trust in her brown eyes. "Is the offer still on the table?" she asked of their fake marriage.

He drew a calming breath and nodded. "It is."

"Logistics to be determined," she added, "But—"

"Macy, what's the holdup? I want to get going," an adult female voice called out from another part of the house.

Macy slid her hand in his. "Let's do this."

Every time Jaxon stepped onto the field, he wrapped himself in his All-Star persona to put on a show. Telling himself this situation was no different, he rolled back his shoulders, squeezed Macy's hand for reassurance, and let her lead the way.

He followed her down a short hall and into a room, stopping at the chaos before him. There were clothes everywhere, no space to walk, with garments hanging out of open drawers and shoes added to the mix on the floor. Tiny lights were strung around the room and outlined a tapestry over the double bed. And like Macy had told him, a huge suitcase sat on the mattress, stuffed full for a much longer time than one night.

A teenager with a pink stripe in the front of her

hair stared at him open-mouthed, and her mother, a woman dressed younger than her years, with heavy blonde highlights, lips with filler, and enough Botox to prevent muscle movement, also stared with obvious recognition in her eyes.

"Macy, what in the world? What is Jaxon Prescott doing here?" the woman asked.

Jaxon lifted their entwined hands, then let go and pulled Macy against him, liking the feel of her soft body against his. "We're engaged."

"What?" Hannah shrieked. "I thought that picture meant it was a one-night hookup. Oh, my God!"

Macy leaned into him, playing the role. "It all happened so fast, but that's what happens with…" She hesitated then said, "Love at first sight."

Lifting Macy's hand, he kissed her knuckles. "It's a pleasure to meet you, Hannah. I've heard a lot about you. And you must be Hannah's mother." He turned to the woman with calculation in her eyes.

"Yes, I'm Lilah." She extended her hand for a dainty shake.

"Obviously you know all about us. But we know nothing about you. Macy, how could you spring this on your sister?"

"I was planning on sitting Hannah down and introducing them this weekend, but you're here, and you said you were taking Hannah for the night, so I called

Jaxon to come over now," Macy explained, not missing a beat.

Lilah glanced between Macy and Jaxon, the wheels obviously turning. She was looking for any angle to help herself or figure out Macy's plan.

"I want to go with Mom."

Macy was unable to hide the full-body flinch her sister's words caused.

"And you can't stop me from taking Hannah." Lilah pulled her daughter closer to her.

"Actually, I *can* prevent you from leaving. I have custody." She glanced at Hannah, her gaze softening. "But I won't as long as you're home in time for dinner tomorrow."

"But—"

"It's called compromise," Macy informed her sister, but Jaxon knew she was communicating with Lilah.

"Fine," the other woman said through clenched teeth.

"Hannah, finish packing. Lilah, a word?" Macy tipped her head toward the door, and Lilah dutifully headed into the hall.

Macy shut the door behind her before either of them spoke.

"Lilah, what is it you want? Responsibility for a teenager can't really be it."

The other woman paused, and for a moment, Jaxon thought she was going to admit to something beyond wanting her daughter back. But he could see the minute she changed her mind and decided to continue her charade, whatever it was.

"I want my child. And I don't know what kind of game you're playing, but marrying a partying baseball player isn't going to win you custody."

"Oh, no? A stable family who can afford to take care of her?"

"Not to mention a safe home with two adults who have her best interests at heart," Jaxon picked up where Macy left off. "We'll be meeting with a lawyer and you can expect a fight."

Ice formed in Lilah's gaze. "A quickie courthouse wedding isn't going to convince a judge you're the right place for Hannah."

Pulling Macy close, he savored her floral scent before he grinned at Lilah. "Who said anything about a quickie courthouse wedding? My bride deserves the best, and that's what she's going to get."

Beside him, he felt Macy stiffen in shock. He was pretty surprised himself, but something about this woman pushed his buttons and annoyed him to the point where he was all in on this wedding and everything it entailed.

He hated to use his wealth to pull strings, but

money bought anything, including the ability to throw a last-minute show that would convince a judge this wasn't a quickie, just-for-custody marriage. With Bri's help and a few phone calls, he could have his entire huge family and all his friends in his house by next weekend, a caterer hired, flowers delivered, and a convincing wedding *would* happen. It might not be as big as his brother's last weekend, but it would have every appearance of reality and true love.

Jesus. Who was he? Go big or go home, he guessed.

"Nobody is going to doubt what we have is real." He'd do whatever he needed to in order to get Macy custody of her sister. Not only did he owe her, she was right. Lilah was a schemer, and he didn't like her trying to take advantage of Macy and her younger sister. The woman wanted something. What, they'd have to figure out together.

Macy rested her hands on his shoulders and leaned in close, surprising him with a kiss on his cheek before glancing at Lilah. "Watch it, Lilah. Jaxon doesn't like to lose. And neither do I."

With a huff, Lilah called out for Hannah, and a few minutes later, they gathered at the door, ready to go.

"Call, text, whatever," Macy said to her sister.

The teenager rolled her eyes and they walked out the door.

* * *

MACY HADN'T REALIZED how much she'd appreciate having someone to share the burden of Lilah with until Jaxon had stood up beside her. He'd been more supportive than she'd anticipated, and now she felt as if she had an ally. Although she worried about bringing Jaxon into Hannah's life and having them bond only to divorce at some point in the future, her current circumstances didn't give her a choice. She'd just have to deal with her disappointment when the time came. She'd probably be equally disappointed herself. Jaxon was a good man, and she was lucky he was willing to step into this mess with her.

"That was crazy," Macy said to Jaxon. "You didn't have to promise a big event just to prove a point."

His gorgeous indigo-colored eyes met hers. "If we're going to do this, might as well do it right. And if it helps us both get what we want out of the deal, then why not?" He grinned, looking more relaxed than she'd expect considering he didn't want to get married any more than she did.

"Why are you so calm?" she asked, her own heart racing.

He shrugged, those muscles working beneath a white tee shirt. "Once I made the decision for a temporary marriage and realized how much it wouldn't just help me but you, too … it felt right. I wasn't going to let my life screw up yours."

She nodded, but he deserved to think things through and know what he was in for. "You do realize I have a huge fight on my hands, right? And now you're involved, too? It's not too late to back out. I know what I'm getting out of this, but are you sure you need to take such a huge step to right past mistakes?"

He nodded. "Believe me when I tell you everyone in my professional life is going to think this is a great idea." He reached up and caressed her cheek, causing a flutter in her belly she was getting used to around him. "And," he continued, "I believe we can make this work for as long as it's practical for us both. When things settle down, we'll quietly and amicably end things."

Her stomach cramped at his words, telling her this was a really bad idea for her heart. Still, knowing what was at stake, she blew out a breath and nodded. "Okay then. Thank you."

She glanced out the window and watched as Lilah's car finally pulled out of the driveway and onto the street. "I don't get it. Lilah is not mother material. The first time she has to say no to Hannah and is faced with a teenage tantrum, Lilah is going to change her mind. In the meantime, she's going to cost me a fortune in legal fees," she muttered. "Speaking of which, you wouldn't happen to know a family law attorney would you?"

"I'll make some calls and come up with someone good."

"Great. I appreciate it."

He put an arm around her shoulder and his warmth felt good. Right. Unable stop herself, she leaned into him, resting her head on his shoulder. Just because Lilah had left her emotionally exhausted, she told herself.

"Let's go sit down and talk," he said.

She led him to the family room with pale peach walls and gray furniture. This room always calmed her. Her favorite reading chair was in here along with a beautiful view of the backyard.

They settled side by side on the sofa, and he pulled her hand into his. "Let's tackle a few issues."

"Such as?"

"We already know we're getting married. I was thinking we could pull my family into it and let Bri work her magic. We could be married by next weekend. Use my house, have it indoors or outdoors, it's up to you."

She managed a nod. She wouldn't mind turning over logistics of the wedding to her best friend and Jaxon's sister. "Okay."

She agreed on a large wedding because it would

look better to a judge if they appeared to be in love and wanting a big family event rather than a quickie courthouse one, as Lilah had mentioned. "What else?"

"For starters, where are we going to live? I'm not trying to insult you, but my place has a lot more room."

She blinked in surprise, realizing how much she hadn't considered. He wanted her to move out of her home? She trembled but understood it made sense. Everything was just happening so fast. And this was just one more thing to readjust to when things ended.

Then something dawned on her. "What about Hannah's school district? It won't be the same." She bit down on her lower lip and paused. "I suppose I could ask for special permission to keep her at her current school. I don't believe they're overcrowded. Hopefully we can make it work."

He nodded. "Good."

"Hannah now knows we're engaged, but I need to have a conversation with her about everything so she understands," she murmured, not looking forward to it. Teenage tantrum to follow, she was sure.

"Do you want me there with you?" Jaxon asked.

He was definitely a good guy. "I appreciate the of-fer, but I think it's best if I talk to her first. Then you two can get to know each other. I'll do it when she gets home tomorrow."

"Okay. Tell her I have a movie theater in the basement, a pool in the backyard, and a basketball hoop if she likes that sort of thing," he said.

"In other words, bribe her like her mother's going to do."

He shrugged. "At this point, whatever works."

Blowing out a deep breath, Macy nodded. He had a point. Macy's father had given them a comfortable life, but he was pragmatic, like Macy. It was no wonder all the makeup and other gifts made Hannah's eyes light up and swayed her choices. Though Macy wanted nothing more than for Hannah to *want* to live with her, she had no doubt Lilah was going to make it a tough fight.

"What about my family?" he asked. "Do you want to be with me when I tell them the news? That way we can get the ball rolling on the wedding planning. My mother is going to lose her mind."

"In a good way, I hope?"

He treated her to a slow grin. "You have no idea. Marrying us off is her life's mission."

Macy shifted in her seat. "And you're about to go from her disappointment to her–"

"Next favorite. I can't beat the first grandchild or the first wedding, but I can come in before Braden and Bri."

He grinned at the realization and Macy rolled her

eyes. "Is everything a competition with you sports types?"

"Yep."

She would laugh except there was a serious component to this. "You do remember this engagement is fake, right?"

His gaze met hers, his expression intent. "About that. Remember what I said about not being celibate?"

She swallowed hard. "How could I forget?" It had been in the back of her mind ever since they'd agreed to get married.

"I want a real marriage." Reaching out, he tucked her hair behind one ear, his rough fingers an aphrodisiac on her skin.

She didn't kid herself that this was a make-or-break decision. He wouldn't marry her if she didn't agree to have an intimate relationship, and considering she'd already slept with him, how could she say no? To do so would be admitting she was afraid she'd fall for him, and she had no intention of giving him that sort of leverage.

Besides, she actually respected him for not wanting to marry and look elsewhere for sex, and she didn't expect him to marry her for an indefinite period of time and be celibate. He'd made it clear that option was off the table.

"Macy?" he asked into the silence she'd created.

She looked into his handsome face and drew a deep breath. "A real marriage works for me."

His smile lit up not just the room but everything inside her. He leaned in close, his intention clear, and she met him halfway, their lips locking together and fireworks exploding between them. At this point, she shouldn't be surprised by their combustible chemistry. But she was.

His tongue swiped over her lips and she let him inside. They clashed and curled, causing her entire being to come alive with need. From a simple kiss, no other parts involved. And boy, did she remember what it was like when the rest of his body tangled with hers and brought her to the height of passion.

Lifting his head, he met her gaze, a sensual smile on his full, gorgeous lips. "It's going to be good between us," he promised. "Really fucking good."

Despite the butterflies flipping through her stomach, she couldn't help but agree. For so long, she'd put her family before her personal life, but she couldn't deny she'd hoped to find a man who could accept the responsibilities that came with her. She'd just never thought he would be a professional All-Star baseball player with a temporary marriage in mind.

T-e-m-p-o-r-a-r-y. No matter how smooth he was with his words and his actions, she needed to remember this wasn't forever.

He was right though. They could make this work for both of them. Sharing a bed with the sexiest man she'd ever laid eyes on wouldn't be a hardship. Not falling for the playboy would be.

Chapter Six

MACY'S HAND SHOOK inside Jaxon's as they approached his mother's house. He couldn't say he was calm, either, but damned if he'd let on. One of them needed to stay cool, and that had to be him if he was going to convince his family they were doing the right thing.

Everyone, from his mom and her boyfriend, Edward, to all of his siblings except Braden, was waiting for them to arrive. He'd called and they'd all agreed to meet here for a surprise announcement.

Jaxon rang the bell and opened the unlocked door. "Don't worry, okay? We're giving them good news. I promise," he told Macy, and together they stepped inside and followed the voices to the family room.

"Jaxon!" His mother called out his name and walked over, pulling him in for a hug.

"Hi, Mom." He embraced her in return.

Christine turned to Macy. "Hi, Macy. This is a surprise."

"She doesn't know the half of it," Macy whispered so low only he could hear.

"I can't wait to find out your news, but I have a surprise for you first. Look who's home!" Christine gestured to the other side of the room, where his brother, Braden, stood, a grin on his face as he met Jaxon's gaze.

He released Macy's hand and crossed the room, giving him a hug and slapping his brother on the back. He hadn't seen Braden since Austin's kidney donation surgery to Uncle Paul. Although unexpected, having Braden here made the night perfect. His whole family would be around for the news. Even Uncle Paul and his significant other, Ron, were here.

"Why didn't you tell me you were coming home?" he asked his oldest brother and Bri's twin, the brother who Jaxon could most relate to. Braden and Bri were thirty-two years old now, and it had been thirteen years since their father passed away. They were nine-teen when he died. But Braden resented Jesse even more than Jaxon, and that was saying something. He'd missed his brother like crazy.

"Isn't a surprise better?" Braden asked.

Jaxon stepped back and looked at his brother, tak-ing in his long hair and scruffy beard. "You look like you just came from the field," he said.

Last he'd heard, his brother was in Sao Paulo, Bra-zil, vaccinating people there. Considering his brother had an adventurous streak, it always calmed him, knowing Braden was in safe places.

"That's because I did. Flew in this afternoon."

Glancing over his shoulder, Jaxon saw his mother was glowing at having her entire family together.

"So what's your news that's going to upstage my homecoming?" Braden grinned, not the type to need to be the center of attention.

Gesturing for Macy to join him, she walked over, his gaze drawn to her fitted white jeans and black tank top that draped over her sexy curves. Despite the look of trepidation on her face, she'd squared her shoulders, obviously bracing herself.

A wedding and short-term marriage might not have been in his plans, but looking at his bride-to-be, he was a lucky man.

He wrapped an arm around her shoulders and pulled her close. "Everyone!" He waited for his family to look his way. "Macy and I are getting married."

"Oh, my God! Another wedding and so soon," Christine said, sounding as excited as Jaxon thought his mother would be. "Macy, welcome to the family!"

"Thank you," she murmured, but Macy, like Jaxon, was obviously aware of the shocked silence surrounding them from everyone else. And then the chaos began, starting with Bri.

"You're what?" his sister asked, eyes wide, mouth open.

"I'm doing what you and Austin wanted. I'm getting married, and I told Macy you'd all be happy for us." He pointedly looked at Bri, warning her to be nice.

His mother pushed her way in and congratulated them both, followed by Braden and Damon, his brothers looking uncertain but keeping their mouths shut.

When the hubbub subsided, Bri stepped over, her eyes narrowed. "You two, come talk to me." She gestured to the sliding glass door leading out to the patio, and they headed outside.

Austin kissed Quinn on the cheek and joined them without being invited, shutting the door behind him.

Bri frowned and spoke before anyone else had a chance. "I told you to get married. We might even have said Macy was the kind of woman you should choose, but I didn't expect you to go out and ask her! And you!" Bri turned to Macy. "What's going on? Don't get me wrong," she said, her voice softer as she spoke to her friend. "If you two were in love, I'd be thrilled, but I don't understand."

"Me neither," Austin said.

"Bri, we know what we're doing," Macy said, sliding her hand into Jaxon's and presenting a united front.

He squeezed her hand back.

"Then explain, please."

Macy blew out a long breath. "As you know, my stepmother is back, and she served me with papers to get custody of my sister, hot on the heels of me being caught doing the walk of shame out of Jaxon's home. I don't trust her or her motives, and a stable marriage and family life with him will help me convince the judge I'm a good parent. That's my reason."

Bri's expression turned to one of compassion. "I am so sorry you're going through this." She touched her friend's shoulder. "But are you sure marrying Jaxon is the solution?"

"It's good for both of us," Jaxon answered for her. "It makes it look like Macy was leaving her fiancé's house, not a one-night stand. And as you both said, marriage and stability will calm management down and help me. It'll make them realize I'm serious about life and I'm not going to do anything stupid again. We're helping each other."

"And you're sure this is what you want? You really want to marry Jaxon?" Bri asked Macy.

"Hey! That almost sounded offensive." Jaxon nudged his sister with his elbow.

"I didn't mean it that way," Bri muttered. "It's just sudden and I'm worried about both of you."

Beside them, Austin just watched in silence.

"And I do," Macy said. "Want to marry him, I

mean. No pun intended." Her light laughter reassured him they were still on the same page.

Austin leaned against one of the light pillars on the corner of the patio. "Sounds like everyone has thought this through."

"We have," Jaxon assured them. "Bri, relax. It's the perfect solution to everyone's problems. Can we count on you to pull a wedding together in a week?" he asked.

"Please? I'll do whatever you need to help," Macy said.

Bri's expression softened. "Anything for you and one of my favorite brothers." She grinned. "If we're going to do this, let's do it right."

"That's what I said." Relief filled him now that his family supported him. "I was thinking of having it at my house, since I have the space inside and out. I'm sure we can get family and friends to come despite it being short notice. I'm just worried about caterers and a photographer…"

"Leave it to me," Bri said. "I have some contacts. We can pull in Faith for desserts," she said of Faith Dare, Ian's half brother's wife who owned a candy shop in New York. She could get them what they needed.

They had a complicated extended family but a loving one. Thanks to Paul, the Precotts had known the

Dares for years, only recently discovering they were family.

"I'll talk to Mom, and between us all, we'll get it done," Bri promised.

"Speaking of Mom, I don't want to set her up for high expectations and hurt her when things come to an end," Jaxon said, not wanting anyone to forget this wasn't permanent.

Austin tapped a finger against his cheek before finally speaking. "I don't think we should put her in the position of having to lie to anyone, either. You're getting married, we don't know for how long, so let it be."

Jaxon nodded. "I agree. Let her enjoy this."

"If you're sure," Macy said, biting down on her lower lip.

"We are," the three of them said at the same time.

Jaxon blew out a deep breath and relaxed.

He had his family on board. Next up? Macy had to convince her sister to move into his house and allow them to become a family.

A temporary one but a family nonetheless.

*   *   *

THE NEXT DAY, Macy tried to go about her time as usual. She hadn't slept well, which didn't surprise her, given all the changes coming up, but she still woke early and walked on the treadmill she'd put in the corner of the den so she could exercise even on broiling-hot Florida days.

She cleaned the house while waiting for Hannah to come home but was interrupted a gazillion times by phone calls from Bri. What kind of flowers did she want at the wedding? Music? Was she available tomorrow to go to a wedding dress shop because she had to buy off-the-rack if she was going to have a gown ready for Saturday? And on and on.

By the time Hannah was due home, Macy was an anxious mess, in part because of the upcoming nuptials, and the more immediate reason was dealing with her sister. Macy had no illusions her talk with Hannah would go as well as their discussion with the Prescotts. After the shock wore off about their engagement, she'd been welcomed to the family and the planning had begun.

Now, however, she had to face her sister when Hannah came home from being with her mother and break the news that they were moving. After Macy finished making her bed, she heard a car door slam outside. Peeking through the window, she watched as her sister pulled her suitcase from the small trunk, waved to Lilah, and headed up the front walk.

Courage, Macy thought to herself. What was the worst that could happen? A teenage tornado temper tantrum, that's all.

She met Hannah in the entryway as she entered the house. Her sister wore leggings and an oversized tee shirt, and her hair was pulled into a messy bun. Along with the suitcase were shopping bags Macy hadn't seen her take from the car. Wonderful, she thought. More attempts by Lilah to buy her daughter's affection.

"How was your night with your mother?" Macy asked, deliberately cheerful.

"Fun! Nobu is so amazing. I had sushi and this awesome dessert." Hannah dropped her bags next to her suitcase, and Macy decided not to bring up the subject of her shopping.

"Can we talk?" Macy asked.

"Yeah. Can you help me bring my stuff to my room?" Hannah picked up the shopping bags, leaving Macy with the heavier luggage.

"Sure thing. Let's go." She followed Hannah across the house and stood the luggage by the closet before sitting on the bed. "Join me. This is important." She patted the comforter on the queen-size mattress.

Warily, Hannah's heavily made-up eyes narrowed as she walked over and eased onto the bed. "Is this about you marrying that baseball player? Mom said you just want his money."

Macy nearly choked on her own saliva. Talk about the proverbial pot calling the kettle black. "Yes, it's about Jaxon. I know this is sudden, but when you get to know him, you're really going to like him. And he has a big family and they can't wait to meet you."

Hannah picked up a ratty old teddy bear she'd had since she was little and set it on her lap, a sweetly amazing contradiction to the hard outer shell she liked to project. "I don't need more family."

"We'll take it slow, okay? But here's the thing." Macy drew a deep breath for courage. "We're going to move in with Jaxon."

"What? No! I'm not leaving my house."

"Hannah, it makes sense. Jaxon's house has more room." She thought about his selling points and, hating herself for stooping to Lilah's level, decided to go for it. "He has a pool and you can invite your friends over to hang out and a movie theater in the basement." She skipped mentioning the basketball hoop, knowing that wasn't appealing to this particular teenage girl.

Hannah's eyes lit up, but a few seconds later, a defiant expression crossed her face. "Mom said you'd try and buy me off."

Macy frowned. "There's no buying you off, Hannah. I have custody. You have to come with me. Which means," she said, drawing a deep breath, "technically you have to switch school districts, but I'm going to work on keeping you where you are now." She said it as fast as she could, before Hannah could have a full-blown fit.

Hannah's light brown eyes shot angry sparks. "I'm not leaving my friends and you can't make me."

Actually Macy could force her to do just that, but she decided not to say so. She had faith she could convince Hannah's current school district to let her remain there, which would allow her to avoid this entire conversation. "Let's not worry about it until we have to. I'll look into it first thing on Monday." She pushed herself to her feet just as Hannah spoke.

"Mom said she wants me to come live with her and it's going to be up to a judge to decide." Hannah flung that barb, hitting Macy in the heart.

What kind of mother told her child she was the center of a custody battle?

Drawing a calming breath, Macy turned to face her sister. "I love you, Hannah. And I want what's best for you. I believe that's living with me. I'm sorry you have to go through this, but everything will work out."

"I want to live with my mom."

Macy gritted her teeth, knowing that sentiment would make her battle that much harder. She opted to ignore the comment and instead changed the subject. "How's pizza for dinner?"

"Whatever."

Yep, life was great. "Unpack and I'll call you when

it's time to eat." She stepped out of the room and shut the door behind her, leaning back against the frame.

How had her life gotten so out of control? An angry teenager who wanted to live with a woman with an agenda Macy hadn't yet figured out, marriage to a man she barely knew on the horizon, and all her energy going into keeping Hannah away from her mother. Macy's dad had been gone for almost a year, but she'd been so busy taking care of Hannah and home, she barely had time for herself. And it didn't look like that would be changing any time soon.

Her cell phone, which she'd tucked into her back pocket, began to ring. She pulled it out, saw Jaxon's name, and her stomach did an immediate flip, a jolt of awareness going through her.

Memories of their joined bodies flickered through her as she answered. "Hello?" She stepped away from the door so she had more privacy.

"Hey. How'd it go with your sister?" he asked, and she found herself touched that he'd bother to ask.

She glanced at the closed door and sighed. "About as well as you'd expect."

"Shit. I'm sorry. But I do have good news. I spoke to my cousin Alex Dare and his wife, Madison. They had a family situation a few years ago, and they recommended a lawyer named Jonathan Ridgeway. I have his name and number and you can call first thing

Monday. I'll text you his information, and we can go to the appointment together."

He stunned her, not just with how quickly he'd gotten the information but by the fact that he was acting the part of the husband she needed. True, they'd agreed to help each other, but she never thought he'd step up so much.

"Thank you! I'm really grateful, and to be honest, I'm going to need the support. Lilah told Hannah she's fighting me for custody. I was hoping to keep it quiet somehow. I don't think Hannah needs any more disruption in her life. Between losing Dad, her mother's sudden appearance—"

"And our marriage," he said in a husky voice.

"Right." She shivered at the reminder.

With his voice in her ear, she couldn't help but think about the fact that she'd soon be in his bed again. Her nipples hardened at the thought, desire and yearning pulsing through her veins. She couldn't deny she wanted him, but she feared how complicated this situation could quickly become if she let her feelings grow along with her desire. She knew he didn't believe in forever, and she couldn't help but wonder why.

She forced herself back to the subject at hand, talking to Jaxon about Hannah. "Oh, and Hannah informed me she wants to live with her mother, so there's that."

Her heart hurt at the thought of her sister choosing her selfish parent over Macy. No matter how much she understood that a child needed to know her mother loved her, Macy just didn't believe that was the case here.

"That really sucks. We'll make her home life good and fun. You can count on that."

She grinned at his attempt to make her feel better. "If I thought Lilah really had Hannah's best interest at heart and was the better choice, of course I'd step aside and just play the role of her big sister."

"I met Lilah and my gut agrees with yours. She's up to something."

"It's good knowing you have my back." She paused and asked, "Want to come by for pizza? You can spend time with Hannah. Just expect her to sulk and be a brat."

"Love to. As a matter of fact, how about I pick it up on the way over?" He answered quickly without taking time to think.

Obviously she wasn't keeping him from other things in his life. On some level, he must want to spend time with her. But she couldn't let herself think that way. Him coming over was to perpetuate the charade of the marriage and help make it work. That was all.

* * *

JAXON'S LIFE HAD changed overnight. Just having made the decision to marry Macy and knowing he now had responsibilities ahead of him had altered his outlook. He was thinking ahead and about things more important than him.

Early this morning, he'd walked around his house and wondered how Macy would feel about the huge mansion he'd bought just because he had the money to spend. There'd been a time when he imagined buying a house like this and living in it with Katie, having kids and a family, something he didn't think about often anymore. But since he was getting married, the ghost of her betrayal came back to remind him that she hadn't thought he was worth the hassle of living his lifestyle. He needed to remember Macy would feel the same way.

He had a home gym in the basement, a movie theater as he'd told her, a massive pool outside, a kitchen a woman who liked to cook would love, and her sister would have her own room. Hell, she'd have her pick of bedrooms.

As for the master, he had two walk-in closets, so Macy would have space of her own, and since they had built-ins, including drawers, he didn't need to make extra space for her. His stomach lurched a bit at the thought of a woman moving in, but knowing it was Macy eased the sting. Until he reminded himself not to get invested any more than he had to.

Bri had called him a bunch of times asking him wedding-reception-related questions, and he'd told her to talk to Macy. This might be a marriage of convenience, but there was no reason she couldn't have the kind of wedding she wanted as long as they could pull it off in a week.

He stopped at his favorite pizza place, picked up a plain and a pepperoni and a few bottles of soda, and headed over to her place as promised. She must have been looking out for him, because she met him at the door and helped him with the boxes.

"Thanks for coming," Macy said with a welcoming smile. "I should warn you Hannah is still in a mood. She might just send you running."

He grasped Macy's hand because she actually sounded worried. "I'm not going anywhere. But I am starving, so let's go inside and eat."

The stress lines around her mouth eased. He followed her into the kitchen, preparing to have his hands full trying to charm a teenager.

As Macy readied the kitchen, he enjoyed the view of her long, tanned legs in a pair of denim shorts and a tee shirt tight enough to accentuate her full breasts. She might not dress up like the women who hung around the stadium and bars, hoping for an easy fuck, but she was a hell of a lot sexier. And he couldn't wait to get his hands on her bare flesh and taste every inch of her skin again. He wasn't used to the anticipation, the wait. The buildup of wanting.

As a Major League player, he could have his pick of women, which was what made this one unique. Yes, she'd slept with him, but in a very real way, he still had to work for it. And he was very much up for the challenge.

Chapter Seven

MACY, HANNAH, AND Jaxon sat in the kitchen, a small room with a table that seated four, light wood cabinets, and matching stone tile. Two pizza boxes were open on the counter, and Macy had had Hannah help her set the table and put ice in their glasses before they'd all gathered to eat. The house reminded Jaxon of the one he'd grown up in with his siblings, but the boys had shared rooms. Bri, of course, had her own domain.

While Macy ate a piece of plain and Jaxon took his second slice of pepperoni, Hannah sat with an empty plate, and Macy seemed content to ignore her and not stir up a fight in front of him.

"Are you sure I can't get you something to eat?" Jaxon asked the teen, whose pout hadn't changed throughout his attempts at conversation.

"I don't like pepperoni," Hannah said, crossing her arms across her chest.

"Then take a slice of plain." Macy's jaw clenched as she held on to her anger. "Tell us about your house," she said to Jaxon, changing the subject.

He got the hint. This was his chance to sell Hannah on the move. "It's way too big for one person, so it's going to be great having you both there. And Hannah, you can have your pick of rooms," he said to the girl who'd been ignoring him all night. "You can redecorate any way you want. Make the room yours."

For the first time all evening, the teenager's eyes showed a glimmer of interest. "I guess that's cool. Until Mom wins custody."

Hurt flashed across Macy's face, and Jaxon couldn't stand by and let Hannah get away with her smart mouth. She had no idea how fortunate she was to have someone who cared and wanted the responsibility of taking care of her. His own life was strange, a father who'd willingly gone through sperm donation by another man to have kids but gone on to treat them with anger and resentment.

"Do you know how lucky you are to have a sister who's been there for you after your mother disappeared?" he asked.

Hannah shook her head, the pink strand whipping across her face. "Mom had to find herself, but she's back now and she wants me."

Ignoring that statement, he cleared his throat and continued to talk to Hannah, not wanting to see the pain in Macy's eyes. "I get what it's like to have a disinterested parent. My dad wasn't my real father, something I didn't discover until last year. And he treated me badly because I didn't want to play football. Baseball wasn't good enough for him, you know? So he treated me like shit," he said honestly. "But I always had my brothers and my sister just like you've always had Macy."

Hannah's eyes opened wide at his revelation. "What about your mom?" she asked. "Where was she?"

"Hannah—" Macy shook her head, obviously not wanting to put him on the spot.

Of course, she didn't know all that much about his past. Yet. He had a feeling they'd be sharing more things as time went on.

"It's fine. I love my mother. She was and is a great parent, but she never really stepped in and stopped my father's verbal abuse about how I wasn't a man if I didn't play football." He shook his head at the ugly memories. "I guess she did the best she could." Short of her leaving Jesse, Jaxon believed that. "All I'm saying is cut your sister some slack and see how much she loves you."

Typical teenager, Hannah didn't say anything in response.

Shocking him, Macy reached across the table and put her hand over his, the gesture hitting him in the heart.

"I'm not hungry." Hannah pushed back her chair, the legs squeaking against the floor.

"Ask if you can be excused, please," Macy reminded her.

With a roll of her eyes, the teen parroted, "Can I be excused?"

Macy nodded. "Put your clean plate back in the cabinet and the silverware away."

With an annoyed groan, Hannah did as she was told, Macy watching her the entire time.

Only when they were alone did she turn to Jaxon. "Now's the time to change your mind." She looked grim, as if she fully expected him to walk away just because her little sister had been a brat.

"I can handle her." Realizing he still held Macy's hand, he squeezed tight. "We're a team now." He truly felt like they could do this and make this crazy short-term marriage work.

For both of them.

She pulled her bottom lip between her teeth and released it. "You stood up for me," she said in obvious awe, making him realize how alone she'd been until now.

Despite his father's treatment of him in the past, as he told Hannah, he'd always had his siblings. His mom. His uncle. A large family he could always turn to. Macy hadn't had that, and as a result, she was tangling with an angry teenage girl alone.

Well, no more. "Hannah needs to understand the value of what she has in you. She doesn't now but she will. Right now, she has her mother's voice in her ear, presents filling the hole that her absence created. Just keep being there. That's the one thing you can give Hannah over time that her mother can't."

"Or won't." Macy toyed with the fork she hadn't used but had set the table with anyway. "It sounded like you understand what it feels like to be an angry teen."

"That's because I do." Instead of the shutters coming down behind his eyes, he allowed her to see the hurt left by his father's words. Letting anyone in was new for him, something he hadn't done since Katie.

"I'm so sorry," she murmured. "No child deserves to be treated as less than anything or anyone."

He rolled his shoulders, telling himself he'd long since accepted his past. "It made me who I am today. And I can't say I'm thrilled with everything I've done, but I know going forward I'm going to get it right. Starting with helping you." His words took even him by surprise.

He'd thought of this spur-of-the-moment marriage as a fix to his problems, but he wanted to help her, too.

Her soft gaze met his. "I'm really grateful. I know Hannah has an attitude, but she's my sister, and beneath the hard exterior is a hurt little girl."

His heart squeezed because he knew how Hannah felt.

"I'm going to make it up to you," Macy said. "I'll be there for you as much as you need. Public appearances, anything that shows your management you're making an effort to change."

Leaning forward, he kissed her forehead, wishing he could turn it into a real, heated make-out session, but not now. Not with Hannah nearby.

Which brought him to another thought he'd had. "So, if Hannah can stay either with her mother or a friend, I want to take a quick weekend honeymoon. Let us really get to know one another," he said in a deliberately husky voice because he couldn't wait to get her naked again.

Macy's eyes opened wide, her pink lips parting in surprise. "Where did you want to go?"

"Our cousin Asher Dare–"

"Why does that name sound familiar?" she asked, wrinkling her nose adorably.

"He owns Dirty Dare Vodka with his brother, Harrison–"

"The movie star?" The shock in Macy's voice amused him. The Dares were an eclectic family owning a variety of businesses, from sports to Dirty Dare Vodka to nightclubs all over the world and more.

"Yes, that Harrison Dare. I like to call them the Dirty Dares. You know because of the vodka company name." He grinned.

"Yes, I got that." Macy laughed.

They were cousins on his New York family's side. "Asher has a private plane and a house in the Bahamas on Windermere Island, which is connected to Eleuthera. Anyway, I gave him a call, and the place is free this weekend. We can leave any time we want after the wedding and come home a day or two later. What do you say?" He hadn't realized how much he wanted her to say yes until he'd asked her to go.

Time alone with Macy in a sexy bikini, with white sand, blue water, hot sun, and cold drinks, away from everyone and the stress of daily life. Once they returned home, responsibilities would keep them busy, but a day or two alone? He wanted that badly.

"I'm not sure I should be leaving Hannah with her mother lurking around right now," Macy murmured.

"We could leave Saturday after the wedding, spend all day Sunday and Sunday night on the island, and we'll be home by the time Hannah gets back from school Monday. Then we'll use the week to move you guys in and everything will be fine. I promise. You deserve at least twenty-four hours to yourself before you come back to reality." And the custody fight she had to deal with kicked in.

She paused and gave it some thought. "Okay." She treated him to a smile that lit him up inside.

"Yeah?"

She nodded.

Unable to resist, he leaned over and pressed his lips to hers, his tongue sliding over her mouth and slipping inside. She moaned and twisted her tongue with his, the kiss deepening. Desire filled him, his cock coming to life, and he knew he wouldn't be getting up from the table any time soon, so he pulled back before they got caught.

"Once we're alone, I'm not stopping." He threaded his fingers through her hair and tugged on the long strands.

Her gaze deepened, and when he glanced down, her nipples were tight against the tee shirt. "When we're alone, I won't want you to stop."

And on that admission, she rose to her feet and began clearing the table, leaving him to wait until his erection eased before he could get up and help her finish up.

*   *   *

MACY OPENED HER front door an hour after Hannah went to school to find Bri standing on her porch.

Dressed not for work but in a casual pair of leggings and a cropped top, she didn't wait to be invited in.

"You and I are going to have a long talk," Bri said, brushing past Macy and heading inside.

Macy shut the door and locked it, then followed her friend into the kitchen. "Coffee?" she asked as Bri plopped her large purse on the table.

"God yes. I need caffeine."

Grabbing two pods, Macy brewed them quick cups of coffee, added almond milk to her own and so did Bri. Then they sat down and Macy waited, because her friend would talk when she was ready.

"You can't fall in love with my brother."

And she was obviously ready. "What the hell are you talking about?" Macy's heart beat harder in her chest at the mere suggestion of her falling for Jaxon. "We have an arrangement and we're in agreement. Getting married works for both of us. No feelings involved."

It was all she could do not to put one hand behind her back and cross her fingers because Jaxon was just so easy to like. Besides his easygoing personality, he went out of his way to help her, and for that she was grateful, and he'd opened himself up to her fifteen-year-old sister, something he hadn't had to do. And he was a sexually dynamic man. The whole package, she mused, her body tingling at the thought of Jaxon

Prescott.

"There! That dazed look on your face. You're thinking about him, aren't you?"

Bri wagged a finger at her and Macy smacked it away. "Cut it out. I can handle your brother and this convenient marriage. It will be fine."

"Good, because given Jaxon's past, he really doesn't believe that someone could love him and stand by him," Bri said. "He's amazing and he doesn't know it. Damn my father for the effect he had on him." She shook her head and her expression grew sad.

"He told Hannah and me that Jesse made him feel like shit because he played baseball instead of football. It sucks to have a parent not support you. He deserved so much better," Macy said in defense of the man who'd done so much for her already.

Bri blinked. "He admitted to that?"

After taking a sip of her coffee, Macy nodded. "He was trying to show Hannah how lucky she was to have had me there for her after Lilah left. Because he knew what it was like to have a parent who wasn't there for him."

Eyes wide, Bri said, "I'm stunned. He never talks about our father or how he treated him." She wrapped her hands around her mug and studied Macy as if she was seeing something new and unique, and Macy squirmed in her seat.

"But Jaxon had those inadequate feelings rein-forced by a woman in his life after Dad, and I just don't want you hurt by having hopes of changing him. Not that I would betray him by explaining. That's between the two of you if he chooses to confide in you."

Macy nodded in agreement, glad her friend hadn't tried to ply her with information about Jaxon's past. "Whatever happened with Jaxon and this other woman, I'd rather hear it from him than you. But I appreciate the warning."

Not that she liked thinking about Jaxon and any other female. The thought caused her stomach to twist in jealous knots. Not a good sign. But she wouldn't admit as much to Bri.

"I just care about you." Bri rose and put her mug in the sink. "I was going to check out a new kickbox-ing class. Want to come?"

"I'd love to." Macy was grateful for the change of subject. "Just let me change and I'll be right back."

She headed for her room, glad Bri had asked her to join her. She needed to exert some energy and get sappy emotional thoughts of falling for Jaxon out of her head.

*   *   *

TUESDAY MORNING, JAXON headed over to the gym

to meet Linc, and after a competitive game of hoops, he showered and dressed in his jeans and a black tee. The locker room was empty, and he glanced at his friend, who was packing up his duffel bag. Throughout the game, Jaxon had gone back and forth on how to tell Linc his news. And now that they were alone, the time had arrived.

"Got any plans now?" Jaxon asked because he had a stop to make and could use some help.

Linc glanced up from zipping his bag, his blond hair falling over one eye. "Nope and I don't have to be home until dinner. Why?"

"Feel like going shopping with me for an engagement ring and wedding band?"

Linc began to choke and Jaxon slapped him on the back.

"Sorry. I thought you said you wanted to go shopping for an engagement and wedding ring," Linc said.

Jaxon couldn't help but grin at his friend's reaction. "Yeah ... well, remember I mentioned Austin and Bri thought me settling down was a good way to calm management and restore faith in me?"

"Yes, but you said no way in hell."

"That was true until I met a woman who needs the stability of marriage, too. A woman I like, have chemistry with, and who agreed to marry my sorry ass." Jaxon picked up his bag and lifted a hand so the duffel hung behind his shoulder.

"Did she also agree to an open marriage? Because I can't see you doing this otherwise. I mean, there's no way you'll marry someone and not get laid."

"Actually she agreed to a real marriage, so that takes care of that." He started for the door when Linc spoke.

"Wait. You're going to be faithful to one woman?"

The shock in his friend's voice would have made Jaxon burst out laughing if someone hadn't walked into the locker room. "Let's take this outside," he said, wanting privacy.

Usually they used the gym at the stadium, but sometimes they didn't want to take the forty-minute ride there and they hit up a local place instead. They strode through the main area where all the equipment was located, passing people who stared at their familiar faces as they headed out into the blazing Miami sun. Luckily no one stopped them for a picture or an autograph.

Jaxon headed to his car and Luke joined him at his vehicle.

"You're serious?" his friend asked, his expression one of disbelief. "Who is it?"

"Damn serious. It's the woman who got caught leaving my house and became a social media sensation."

"A groupie?" Linc asked, disgusted.

Jaxon shook his head. "Hell no. She's special. Macy is smart, gorgeous, and she's got her hands full with her fifteen-year-old sister."

Linc had narrowed his gaze at the word *special*. Jaxon picked up on that and realized his slip. But it was true. Still, better he stuck to the facts.

"The kid's mother wants her back after being an absentee parent, and being splashed all over the internet is going to hurt Macy's case. Us getting married will give her a solid family situation in order to help win custody. And we know management will be relieved I'm settling down."

Linc dropped his bag onto the ground. "Let me get this straight. You're going from a bachelor who fucks anything that walks to a guy with a kid. Overnight."

"You're a dick. But that about sums it up. I'm going to get my life together." He wanted that. Having dinner with Macy had been nice. Normal. And he wanted to help her with Hannah. He also desired to get her back into bed. "That's the plan and I believe we can help each other. Not to mention it's good for me to focus on something other than myself."

"Wow." Linc stared at him for a long while. "Why do I get the feeling you really like this girl?"

Jaxon shrugged, thinking of the simple meal in her small kitchen, the way she wanted to help her sister, and her beautiful brown eyes. "Because I do. Now will you help me pick out rings?"

Although this was a marriage of convenience, he and Macy would be together for a prolonged period of time, and he wanted her to have a ring suitable for the wife of a Major League Baseball player.

"And will you come to the wedding on Saturday at my house?" he asked before Linc had even replied about ring shopping. "There'll be an evite in your email later today. Bri's at the top of her game."

"Jesus. You're serious." Linc ran a hand through his hair. "Lizzie isn't going to believe this," he said of his wife. "Okay, sure. Make sure you sign a prenup," he reminded him.

"Austin already has it in the works. Called me first thing this morning. I don't anticipate a problem in that area. Macy isn't with me for my money. She wants the same things I do. Marriage and stability."

Linc stared. "Every woman you've ever been with wanted your money."

"Macy doesn't and you'll see that once you meet her. I'll drive to the jewelry store and bring you back to your car afterwards."

A couple of hours and many thousands of dollars later, Jaxon had a Tiffany ring in his pocket that he hoped would fit, matching wedding bands with a promise they'd be sized properly by Friday, and he dropped off his still-stunned best friend back at the gym where they'd started.

Once he was alone, he picked up the phone and called Bri on the audio of his car while driving to Macy's house.

She answered on the first ring. "Hey, bro. Everything good?" she asked.

He pulled onto the highway as he replied, "It is. I bought rings, so I'm trying not to panic, but I'm okay."

Bri grumbled something, then said, "Just don't hurt her."

"I don't plan on it," he said, offended. "Give me some credit, will you?"

"This is just out of your depth and I'm worried about both of you," Bri said with a sigh.

"And I appreciate it but everything will be fine. Except for one thing. I was thinking about what a big family we have and how she just lost her dad a short time ago. What can I do to make this easier for her?"

"Aww, you have a heart. Who knew?" His sister laughed, teasing him as he was used to. "But seriously. That's so sweet. And true. Well, we can get Uncle Paul to walk her down the aisle if she's open to it, and maybe I can talk to Hannah and find something from Macy's mom so she has something old. I know Hannah's not always an easy kid, but let me give it a shot."

"Do you have her number?" he asked.

"Umm, no."

He could figure that out. "I'm headed there now. I'll find a way to talk to her. Either ask myself or get you her phone number."

He flipped on his signal and took the exit off the highway to Macy's house. "Thanks for everything. I know how hard you're working to pull this off. And I know I forced us into this situation, but it's going to help Macy, too."

Bri was quiet for a moment, then said, "You're just full of surprises lately."

"Meaning?"

"Oops, I have another call. Have to run. Talk to you soon, Jax. Love you," she said and disconnected them.

"Women," he grumbled to himself. Half the time they never made sense.

He finally pulled into Macy's driveaway, happy he didn't see the red sports car that belonged to Lilah. For what he had planned, he didn't need any more of an audience than necessary.

Chapter Eight

BY TUESDAY, MACY was in full wedding-planning mode courtesy of Bri. Because it was easier, Macy followed her directions in between fitting in design work for clients. Yesterday she'd met Bri at a bridal shop where, somehow, they found an off-the-rack gown she loved along with bridesmaids' dresses for Hannah, Bri, and two other close friends of Macy's, who were scratching their heads at her sudden wedding but thrilled she was marrying Jaxon Prescott.

Macy kept their reasons for the marriage to his family only. They couldn't risk anyone slipping with the secret that it wasn't a truly legitimate union. They both had too much to lose.

To her amazement, Hannah had been an angel at the dress shop, probably because she had her choice of whatever she could buy, also off-the-rack due to no time for many alterations. Luckily for Macy, her sister liked clothes, dresses, and had a blast at the store.

The upcoming big day held a bittersweet quality for Macy. She wasn't a girl who'd dreamed of her wedding her entire life, but she'd never imagined one of pure convenience, either. Added to that, she'd lost her mom years ago and her dad was also gone. While Jaxon would have a huge family surrounding him at their wedding, she'd be feeling very much alone. Her throat filled, as she missed her father more than ever, but she was pragmatic and knew she couldn't change things. She needed to focus on the present.

Speaking of, first thing Monday, she'd called the school district and confirmed that she could keep Hannah in her current school once they moved in with Jaxon. Knowing things would stay the same had calmed Hannah down a lot and eased the growing tension between them at least for now.

She'd also called the lawyer Jaxon had given her, and she had an appointment on Thursday to discuss the custody suit and the situation with Lilah. She was busier than ever and trying not to panic over the fact that she was getting married and going on a honeymoon with the sexiest man she'd ever met and moving into his house soon after.

Hannah was in her room doing homework and chilling out for a change, which gave Macy a chance to sit down and just breathe. Except no sooner had she settled into her favorite chair than the bell rang.

With a sigh, she rose and walked to the door. Looking outside, she was shocked to see Jaxon standing on her front porch.

After unlocking the door, she let him in, immediately wishing she'd looked in the mirror first. Where he wore a pair of fitted jeans and a black tee shirt that showed off the muscles in his chest, arms, and legs, she had on a tee shirt dress with no bra, her hair pulled up in a messy bun, and no makeup.

Way to impress the hot man you're about to marry, she thought wryly. "Jaxon, I wasn't expecting you. Is everything okay?"

"It is. I just wanted to stop by for a few minutes." He ran a hand over his hair and groaned. "Okay, look. Nothing about us is traditional, but if I'm getting married, I want my wife to have a ring."

Only then did she notice he'd had a blue Tiffany bag behind his back that he now held out for her to take. She accepted the gift and, with shaking hands, pulled out a blue box with a white bow.

"Go ahead. Open it," he urged.

She untied the ribbon, lifted the box, and pulled out a velvet case. He took it from her and popped it open, turning the case toward her.

She was unable to take her eyes off the huge diamond staring back at her, and her mouth ran dry. "It's fake, like the engagement, right?" she asked only half jokingly because she didn't know what she would do with a ring this big. She wasn't used to a life of luxury.

Looking into his eyes, though, she realized she'd

hurt his feelings. He'd gone out of his way to buy her a ring, and she didn't mean to seem ungrateful.

"I'm sorry. I didn't mean anything by it. I just didn't expect you to really buy me a ring, let alone a Tiffany one. It's gorgeous, Jaxon, it really is."

He pulled out the ring and held it in his big hand. "If you don't like it, we can get you something else."

"No! I mean, I love it. You just took me off guard, that's all," she said, softening her voice. What woman wouldn't adore this ring? Of course, she wouldn't keep it after the marriage ended. That would be all kinds of wrong, but the fact that he'd thought of buying it at all was touching.

This man constantly surprised her, from backing her up with Hannah the other night to insisting on a big wedding and real marriage, and now with the ring. He wasn't the arrogant playboy he wanted people to think he was based on his past behavior. He was a good guy, a decent man, and he cared about what she thought, felt, and wanted. She almost wished his public persona was the real Jaxon Prescott. He would be so much easier to resist.

"Let's see if it fits."

She held out her hand, grateful for the manicure she'd had last week, and he slid the ring onto her finger.

"A little snug but better than big. I'd die if I had to

worry about losing it," she said, wiggling her fingers. "God, Jaxon, it's incredible."

He blew out a relieved breath. "I'm glad you like it. So officially, Macy Walker, will you marry me?"

"Considering I already bought the dress, yes." She met his gaze and grinned.

He held her hands in his. "Did you know that you have an amazing smile?"

She blinked in surprise, feeling his compliment straight down to her toes.

"And I like kissing your sexy lips," he said in a gruff voice.

She liked him kissing her, too. "You don't say?" Her pulse began a rapid beat and excitement built up inside her chest.

His slow smile evidenced his intent as he moved in close, his mouth hovering over hers. Before she could back out, she rose and met his lips with hers. Still feeling the heaviness of the ring on her finger that marked them as a couple, she parted her lips, and soon their tongues touched, tangled, and sparks flew throughout her body.

He wrapped an arm around her waist and yanked her roughly against him, the hard lines of his chest pressing against her softer curves. Her stomach twisted with desire, and he clearly felt the same, because his hand cupped the back of her head, and he held her tightly against him as his mouth devoured hers.

With a growl, he moved his lips, kissing his way down her jawline to her ear, nuzzling the sensitive skin, making her tremble, and her nipples rubbed against his chest, arousing her even more. He worked his way back up to her mouth, their lips joining once more.

"Eew! Get a room! Is this what I'm going to have to live with?" Hannah stomped into the hallway, making her presence known.

Though Macy attempted to pull back, Jaxon kept a firm grip on her waist. "I just brought your sister her ring. Want to see?"

Some of the irritation left Hannah's expression, replaced by definite interest. "I guess," she said begrudgingly.

Macy stepped away from Jaxon and this time he let her go. She approached her sister, holding out her hand for Hannah to see.

"Holy shit, that's one huge rock!"

"Hannah, that's rude!" Macy chastised but Jaxon merely laughed.

"It is, isn't it?"

She shot him an annoyed glare. Condoning Hannah's behavior wasn't going to do them any good. But she had to admit his method worked, because a grin lifted her sister's lips.

"Wait until my friends see this ring. It's all over school, you know. That you're marrying Jaxon Prescott. It's making me a big deal." Hannah sounded impressed and Macy wanted to lecture her sister on the difference between real and fake friends, but before she could speak, Jaxon did.

"I know the attention must be cool," he said, walking over and putting a hand on Hannah's shoulder. "But the truth is, you want friends who like you for you, not the ones who want to be around you because your sister is marrying a pro baseball player."

Macy would have said the same thing, but Jaxon's gentler voice seemed to reach Hannah in a way Macy was having trouble doing lately.

Hannah blinked and nodded. "I get it. Because all of a sudden Hailey Claiborne and Victoria Mason are paying attention to me and including me at lunch." Hannah bit down on her lower lip. "I've been leaving my best friend, Ruby, to eat with them. I guess that's not cool, huh?"

Jaxon shook his head. "Nope. Not cool."

Amazed at how easily he'd reached her sister when Macy had been struggling, she just stared at the two of them in shock.

"But the guys are talking to me, too. That's okay, right?" She looked up at Jaxon with something akin to hero worship.

"It is … as long as they treat you with respect and aren't just being nice to you in order to get to meet me, only to dump you after. That said, once you're settled at my place, you could have a few friends over, if it's okay with your sister."

Hannah looked at Macy with longing in her eyes. Though she wished this was a conversation she'd been prepared for, she understood how quickly it had come up and how huge it was that Hannah was revealing things about her life to Jaxon. Macy wasn't about to blow it now.

"It's fine. I already said you could have friends over, so it's all good."

"The guys, too?" Hannah asked, a tinge of disbelief in her voice.

"Outside at the pool." Not in the movie theater basement. Macy had to draw the line somewhere, and as long as she could see what was going on, she'd agree.

Besides, this conversation had sidetracked Hannah from thinking about catching Macy and Jaxon kissing, and that was a plus.

"Yes!" Hannah fist-pumped her approval.

"Have you started packing?" Jaxon asked.

Not that he knew it, but Macy had put suitcases in Hannah's room, which she'd deliberately ignored and left empty against the wall.

"I'm going to start tonight." She sheepishly met Macy's gaze, knowing how nasty she'd been about moving. "After I call Ruby and apologize."

"Perfect," Macy said with a smile. Jaxon had worked miracles, and she wasn't about to argue with success.

"Hannah, what do you say we exchange phone numbers, and if you have any questions about the house or your room, you can call and ask me."

Her eyes opened wide and her phone was in her hand in an instant. They made the number exchange, and Hannah beamed, grinning from ear to ear.

And as Macy watched Jaxon earn her sister's trust, she lost the first piece of her heart to Jaxon Prescott.

*   *   *

JAXON HAD TO admit he admired his technique. Getting Hannah's phone number had been easier than he thought but only because he'd bonded with the teenager. He understood Hannah on a level very few people could. Between his uncle Paul, who owned the Miami Thunder, and his brother Austin, who'd been an All-Star wide receiver, he knew what it was like to be used for who you knew. The idea of anyone taking advantage of Hannah in any way pissed him off and turned his stomach. If she was going through a rough patch with Macy, the very least he could do was provide support and understanding while they were a family.

The word *family* didn't choke him as much as he'd have thought. It helped that Macy beamed at him, obviously pleased with how he'd handled her little sister, and a part of him puffed up, knowing she saw him in a positive light.

Hannah had headed to her room, supposedly to start packing, and now he sat in the kitchen while Macy prepared dinner, a roast chicken, red potatoes, and broccoli topped with Parmesan cheese. She'd already invited and convinced him to stay.

As she easily moved around the room, they'd talked about Bri's wedding ideas and laughed at how easily they'd both agreed to her plans. In Macy's case, she said she didn't want to be difficult and there was nothing her friend had proposed that she'd disliked, and for Jaxon, he knew better than to argue when Bri was in tornado mode.

"I need to bring up something awkward," Macy said while the chicken roasted in the oven. She sat down beside him at the island on one of the barstools beside him.

"Go for it."

She swallowed hard. "I want to sign a prenup. I don't want anything from you and I don't want you to think I do."

Her words took him off guard. Yes, he was having a legal document prepared despite believing she wasn't in this for a money grab, but for her to bring it up first? To confirm his gut feelings? That said something about her character and reinforced what he'd thought about her all along.

"Macy—"

"Wait. I need to say this. Please." She met his gaze and he saw serious intent, so he nodded, and she went on. "I realize we're each getting something out of this marriage, but it's not financial for me. Okay, there's some financial gain, obviously. I mean, we'll be living with you and—"

"Hold on." Seeing she was working herself up, he held out a hand. "Yes, we'll sign a prenup. I have one in the works, but I'm going to make sure you and Hannah are taken care of when the marriage ends. It's not like I can't afford it, and you're doing something for me in all this, too."

She leaned closer, elbow on the counter. "Are you sure? Because it's beginning to feel very one-sided."

"I am absolutely positive. This morning, I received a call from my coach. He wanted to congratulate me on my upcoming marriage and to let me know how pleased upper management was to know I was settling down and my *playboy and hopefully brawling* days were over," he said, using air quotes around the words. "So believe me when I say this situation is very equal."

She blew out a relieved breath. "I'm glad to hear we're on the same page. And you really don't have to give us anything when things end."

Why did it bother him to hear her mention things being short-term? That was the point, after all. Pushing the gnawing feeling in his gut aside, he kept things light. "You're going to learn that I usually get what I want. So don't argue, okay?"

She smiled. "Okay. Do I need a lawyer to look over the paperwork?"

"It wouldn't hurt. You should always have someone taking care of your personal interests. Speaking of lawyers, did you call Johnathan Ridgeway about the custody case? I'm sure he can handle the prenup, too." He lowered his voice so Hannah wouldn't hear.

She nodded. "I have an appointment on Thursday at ten a.m."

"I'll be there."

She shook her head. "You don't have to go out of your way for me."

"In this together, remember?" Reaching out, he squeezed her hand, enjoying the feel of her soft skin and remembering the taste of her mouth and lips.

Her fingers tightened around him. "Stop looking at me like that," she whispered.

"Like what?" he asked in a gruff voice.

"Like you want to jump me right now."

His entire body was rigid with desire, the need for her surpassing what he normally felt when he wanted a woman. Which struck him as odd. Different. Because he was used to the kind of female who overdid everything from her hair to her makeup and whose voice always held a come-on.

Not Macy. She was who she was, no artifice or pretense, although she wasn't wearing a bra and he'd had to do his best to ignore her perky nipples showing through her dress. But the fact remained, he wanted her more than he'd ever desired another woman. Warning bells went off in his brain. Again he got the feeling this fake marriage wasn't going to work out exactly as he'd planned.

So when she noted his lust-filled look? Well, she was right. "What if I do want to jump you right now?"

She ran her tongue over her bottom lip, and he followed the movement, his cock rising as she licked.

"Then I'd tell you that you have to wait until our wedding night," she said in a taunting voice.

"Tease."

"Not usually. You seem to bring out the lighter, more fun side of me."

He grinned. "Glad to hear it. Because you bring out the lighter side of me, too."

"So we're a good pair." At the very least, his new life wouldn't be boring, he thought as she called her sister down for dinner.

*   *   *

THE NEXT COUPLE of days flew by, and soon Macy was walking into the lawyer's office downtown. Jaxon had insisted on picking her up and accompanying her to hear what Jonathan Ridgeway had to say about the legal process and her chances for custody of her sister. He also explained that he'd possibly have to testify before the judge, and the more he knew, the better prepared he'd be. He wasn't wrong.

Macy was nervous about what the lawyer might say. Despite Macy being a blood relative, Lilah was Hannah's mother, and Macy knew how much weight that status carried. But she had every intention of fighting because she understood Hannah needed stability in her life, and Macy knew she could provide it for her. Much more so than Lilah.

As they followed a secretary to a conference room with a dark wood table and comfortable-looking chairs, Jaxon slipped his hand into hers, and she squeezed tight, needing the reassurance.

A good-looking man greeted them. With dark brown hair and green eyes, wearing a European-cut suit, he looked the epitome of a high-powered attorney.

"Ms. Walker?" he asked.

"Call me Macy, please." She held out her hand and he shook it. "And this is—"

"Jaxon Prescott," he said, obviously recognizing him, not to mention he'd been the main referral. "It's a pleasure!" The men exchanged handshakes as well. "Alex and Madison are good friends. I already read the papers you forwarded to me, but I want to hear it from you. What can I do for you?" he asked.

Jaxon tipped his head, deferring to Macy. "She'll explain."

"Let's sit." Gesturing to the chairs, Jonathan pulled out one for Macy, and Jaxon made sure to settle in beside her.

When they were all seated, she began, explaining how her father had married Lilah and they'd had Hannah. How Lilah had found being a parent a nuisance and that she'd ultimately left with a wealthy single guy she'd been cheating on her father with, leaving her daughter behind.

"Five years passed with maybe one email and a birthday card, and then she shows up driving a sports car and taking Hannah shopping for all sorts of things she doesn't need to buy her love and affection. And because I'm the person who gives her rules and guidance, she's always mad at me."

Jonathan remained silent for long enough to make Macy anxious. "It's bad news, right?"

He rolled a pen between his palms. "Taking away parental rights is tough."

"Even though she signed her rights away to my dad and he named me as Hannah's guardian in his will?" She gripped the arms of the chair and nearly leapt out of her seat, but Jaxon grabbed her hand, and she knew he was trying to calm her down.

Pulling in a deep breath, she tried to relax in the seat. "Okay, I'm listening."

"I think we can use all of your stepmother's past actions as proof of her inability to give Hannah a stable home. That's the premise of our argument. I understand you two are getting married?"

"In two days. And then they're moving in with me," Jaxon said. "We'll be a family and give Hannah the stability she needs. We're bonding," he said proudly.

Actually they were. After Jaxon had left the other night, all Hannah could talk about was how cool Jaxon was and how she couldn't wait to see his house and bring her friends over. Which bothered Macy on one level, because she didn't want to buy her sister any more than she liked Lilah attempting to do it.

"We're going to have to fight the perception of a quickie marriage after you were served custody papers."

"It's a real marriage," Jaxon said. "If you ask Hannah after living with us, she'll tell you the same thing. We'll be sharing a room. We're a couple." He squeezed her hand tighter.

And though she didn't want to lie to her lawyer, she realized everything Jaxon had told him was the truth.

Jonathan nodded. "Okay, look. I'd like to meet with Hannah, too, though it can wait until after the wedding. I'm sure the judge is going to want to ask her who she would prefer to live with, and at fifteen, that could hold sway."

Macy hadn't seen that coming. "Oh, my God. She's going to say she wants to live with her mother. I'm going to lose my sister!" Jumping up, Macy began to pace in a full-blown panic, and Jaxon stood and wrapped an arm around her.

"You don't know that. Give Hannah time to adjust to your new living arrangements, and she's going to love it. She'll want to stay with us."

"He's right," the lawyer said. "We have plenty of time before the custody hearing in three weeks. Use it wisely. In the meantime, would you agree to hiring an investigator to look into Lilah and see if we can uncover more to back up our claim that she's an unfit parent?"

God, Macy thought. Between the lawyer fees and private investigator cost, this could eat up everything she had. "Do it," she said. Keeping Hannah was worth anything she had to spend.

Jonathan smiled. "Good. As for the prenup agreement you had sent over earlier in the week, you're good to sign. I'm sure you've read it, too, and it's more than fair to you."

"Thank you."

He rose to his feet and shook her hand. Beside her, she felt Jaxon's steady presence and support. No matter what happened, she would be eternally grateful to him.

As they started for the door, Jaxon turned to Jonathan and whispered something Macy couldn't hear, and together she and Jaxon walked out of the office.

Macy waited until they were on the street before drawing in a deep breath of air. Jaxon placed a hand on her back and waited for her to calm down before pulling her into his arms. "It's going to be okay. Trust us together, okay?"

She nodded into his shirt, noting how good he smelled. How warm and masculine. She wanted to burrow into him and stay there.

Instead she let reality intrude. Lifting her head, she asked, "What did you say to Jonathan before we left the office?"

He hesitated before answering. "I told him to bill me."

She shook her head. "No. I can't let you do that. It's my custody fight and–"

"It won't make a dent in my life. I know how that sounds but it's true, so if I can help you, just let me. Please."

She swallowed hard. "I don't like the idea of taking charity."

"Then don't look at it that way. I'm your husband, or I will be, and there's no reason I can't pay."

She stared into his gorgeous eyes and sighed. "I'll make it up to you, somehow."

He reached out and stroked her cheek with his knuckles. "Don't sweat it, okay?"

Easy for him to say, but how could she not be grateful for his generosity? "Okay. Thank you." She flung her arms around his neck and hugged him tight.

"You're welcome."

She tipped her head back, met his gaze. Something serious passed between them, and in that instant, his lips came down on hers. She'd more than grown used to kissing him, and every time she did, she got lost in his taste, his scent, and the hard feel of his body against hers. Just knowing that in two days she'd be his wife and in his bed again set her nerve endings on alert.

The honk of a car startled her, and she jumped, breaking them apart.

"Hey, Jaxon!" someone called out.

The person waved their cell phone at him. "Great picture!" the guy called before jogging off, leaving them staring after him.

She felt the heated blush rise to her cheeks. "Oh, my God. We were caught making out. Again."

Jaxon pulled her against him and kissed the top of her head. "Get used to it. At least now it'll be a photo of me and my fiancée," he said, treating her to his most charming grin. "Not to mention it's proof of a real marriage. It's all good."

He seemed so certain they could make this work she couldn't help but believe him herself.

Chapter Nine

J AXON, HIS BROTHERS, and some of his cousins gathered in one of the downstairs bedrooms of his house in their tuxedos, waiting for the wedding to begin. He'd ceded the master to Macy and the women, knowing they needed more room than the guys.

As much as he'd been outwardly calm in the days leading up to the ceremony, inside there'd always been a level of fear he hadn't admitted to often. He'd been busy calming Macy, but he hadn't confessed to his family or friends how nervous he was about this wedding. He wasn't as much worried he'd miss his bachelor lifestyle as he was panicked that he wouldn't. That he'd end up enjoying family life only to somehow have it ripped out from under him the way it had been before.

He paced back and forth across the floor, ignoring the joking of the other men in the room, his stomach churning with nerves.

"Hey." Austin strode over and, in big-brother mode, put an arm around Jaxon's shoulders. "It's not too late to change your mind."

Jaxon stared in disbelief. "This from the man who thought of the solution?"

"I didn't really think you'd go out and get married," he said somewhat sheepishly. "I just wanted you to calm the fuck down. Don't get me wrong, though. I like Macy."

"So do I." Jaxon liked her a lot. And it had been easy to lose himself in her problems this week and feel like the hero helping her out, first with her sister, then with the lawyer. Somehow he'd managed to put aside the specifics of what it meant to get married and what the repercussions could be.

"And it's not permanent, so relax." Austin gripped Jaxon's shoulder.

"You're right." He blew out a breath. "It's just like any game. Know the rules, play your best, and take the win when it's over."

"You've got this."

He nodded, knowing he did and wondering how Macy was handling her last few minutes of being single.

*   *   *

MACY GLANCED OUT the window at the beautiful setup for her wedding, still shocked she'd reached the point where she was getting married. Jaxon had graciously given up his bedroom as her bridal suite, where she and her bridesmaids were putting finishing touches on their hair and makeup.

"Macy?"

She turned at the sound of Hannah's voice. Her sister looked beautiful, her blonde hair in long spirals, the pink color looking pretty, the light makeup giving her face a rosy glow. The bridesmaids were in purple and lavender dresses, whatever blending color they could find in their size, again, off-the-rack.

"What's up, Hannah? Are you okay?" Macy knew this day would cause them both upheaval.

"Umm, Jaxon called and asked me to find you something from your mom. So you'd have something old and something from your mother. I went through your jewelry. Don't be mad," she said quickly. "And I found this pearl bracelet. I know you didn't plan to wear it, but I thought it would look pretty. And mean something to you." Hannah held out a triple-strand pearl bracelet with a thin diamond clasp.

A lump rose in Macy's throat. With both her parents gone, it hadn't dawned on her to wear something of her mother's, and it should have. Now she'd have a piece of them with her, since her dad had bought the bracelet for an anniversary gift.

"Oh, Hannah, that's so thoughtful!" She accepted the bracelet.

"It was Jaxon's idea," Hannah reminded her,

something Macy had already processed and tucked away in her heart.

"Would you help me hook it on?" She held out her hand, and Hannah placed the strands around her wrist.

From behind her, Bri cleared her throat. "He has his moments." She was obviously talking about her brother.

Macy smiled, more touched than she could say. "Yes, he does."

A knock sounded on the door and Macy called, "Come in!"

Jaxon's uncle Paul, who was walking Macy down the aisle, stuck his head in. "Everyone ready?"

Macy nodded. As ready as she'd ever be.

Everything next was a blur. The bridesmaids and groomsmen lining up. The music causing her stomach to flutter with nerves. Them walking down the aisle ahead of her.

Then, hooking her arm into Paul's, she readied herself to take the stroll down the aisle to the handsome, sexy man in a tuxedo waiting for her at the end.

And that was what she held on to – Jaxon's reassuring gaze and the hot way he appraised her.

"That's the expression of a man in love," Paul said to her quietly.

"What?" Love? No. This was an arrangement, but she couldn't tell Paul that.

Even if a part of her wished his words were true, she understood reality and took that first step, gliding to his side. She passed everyone in the audience staring at them, even a bored-looking Lilah, whose invitation had been to appease Hannah, nothing more.

Jaxon grasped her hands and he grounded her. "You look spectacular," he said softly. "Gorgeous."

Her stomach tumbled over at his words. "Thanks. You're pretty hot yourself."

He grinned just as the ceremony started. She wasn't sure how much time passed when they were pronounced husband and wife. "You may kiss the bride."

Jaxon's eyes locked with hers, he wrapped his arm around her waist, and everything nervous inside her calmed to be replaced with pulsing desire that only he caused.

His lips came down on hers, and he tilted her backwards, putting on a show for everyone in the audience. But all she could focus on was his strength and his perfect kiss, his tongue swiping over her lips and gliding inside her mouth too briefly. Straightening her to a standing position, he held on as everything spun around her.

"Are you good, Mrs. Prescott?" he asked at last.

Her equilibrium restored, she nodded. "All set, Mr. Prescott."

They walked back down the aisle and the guests clapped in celebration. Afterwards, the blur of time continued, dancing, eating, smiling, and talking to family and friends, and at some point they'd gotten separated.

"I wish you the best," Bri said, her indigo eyes, similar to her brother's, matching her purple dress.

"And I appreciate it, you know that."

From across the room, Macy heard Hannah's voice. "I don't understand. You said I could sleep at the hotel with you!"

Macy winced. "Sounds like there's an issue. I've got to go see what's going on."

Before she made it halfway across the room, Jaxon was back by her side. "Hannah sounds upset."

She nodded and together they approached. While Macy was to be on her honeymoon, Hannah had planned to stay with her mother for the weekend instead of with a friend. Despite not wanting to do it, Macy had given Hannah the choice, again trying to seem reasonable prior to dealing with a judge.

"What's wrong?" Macy asked.

"Mom said I can't stay with her while you're gone. Something came up."

Macy narrowed her gaze. "It's two nights, Lilah. The plans are made."

"And something came up that can't be changed."

"Come on, Hannah. Let's go call a friend and get you settled," Jaxon said, leaving Macy to deal with Lilah.

"Really? This is how you show your daughter you love her? And you spring it on us at the last second when we're leaving soon?" Macy's blood roared in her ears. "Are you trying to make things more difficult?"

Lilah shook her head. "Life happens, Macy. It can't be helped."

"Care to fill me in on what suddenly came up that's more important than taking Hannah?"

"Not really," she said between sips of champagne. "It's my business."

That Macy hoped Jonathan Ridgeway would uncover. In the meantime, she needed to make sure Hannah was safe for the weekend, but before she could go looking for her sister and Jaxon, they returned.

"All set. Ruby's mom is going to pick Hannah up before you and I leave," Jaxon said, a reassuring smile on his face.

"All good, Hannah?" Macy asked.

She nodded, looking at her mom through hooded eyes.

"I'll make it up to you next weekend," Lilah promised.

"We may be busy moving. We'll have to let you

know," Macy said, then turned to her sister. "Come on. Let's make sure your bags are ready," she said, despite knowing Hannah was set to go. She wanted to separate her and Lilah.

Hannah remained silent, obviously hurt by her mother's actions, and Macy wouldn't be around to make it better. But she wasn't giving up a honeymoon with Jaxon. Once Hannah got involved with her friend, she'd be fine and busy.

"I have no doubt it's a man that's got Lilah tied up," Macy muttered to Jaxon.

He nodded. "I already texted the lawyer. Don't worry. We're on top of it," he said as if they were a team, and she was beginning to feel like they were. "By the way, I hope it's okay, but I arranged to have yours and Hannah's things moved to my house while we're gone. I don't want you to have to stress about it."

Despite warning herself not to get used to the feeling of being taken care of, she couldn't deny she needed him now. "Thank you. I appreciate it."

After getting Hannah settled and out to her friend's car, Macy turned to Jaxon. "I thought I'd change before we left."

His gaze darkened. "I was kind of hoping to peel you out of that sexy dress." Those gorgeous eyes slid over her, causing her nipples to tighten and her panties to grow wet.

"It's a little crazy to travel in formal wear."

"Just make sure I can peel you out of your clothing and I'll be a happy man."

Desire pulsed inside her, and she merely nodded, unable to speak or respond, realizing for the first time she was in for a sexy, erotic weekend unlike any she'd experienced before.

*   *   *

HOURS LATER, MACY and Jaxon stepped off Asher Dare's private plane into the heat of the Bahamas. Though Florida and Windermere Island had similar weather, the plane had been chilled, and Macy was immediately hit by the humidity and heat. Luckily, she'd changed into a pair of fringed cutoff shorts and a loose but cropped top so she could handle the weather.

The ocean, which she'd seen as the plane dipped and readied to land, was pure blue with pale white sand. Utterly beautiful, it was paradise, and she instantly relaxed, knowing she had two full days to do nothing but enjoy.

To her surprise, Jaxon held her hand as they deplaned, and a car service waited to take them to the house, a white mansion with a huge veranda encircling it. The house sat directly on the beach. Given the fact that Asher Dare was a billionaire, this didn't surprise her. He'd been at the wedding, but she hadn't had time to get to know him.

A butler – yes, a butler – carried their bags up to the room, and once he was gone, Jaxon gestured for her to step into the hall. Curious, she joined him, only to have him scoop her into his arms. She grasped him around the neck, holding on tight, as he carried her over the threshold.

"Jaxon!" She couldn't help but giggle at the silly, romantic gesture.

"Since I won't ever be doing this again, might as well get it right the first time."

He spoke without thought, and she pushed away the pain in her chest upon hearing his words. He wasn't telling her anything she didn't already know or that they hadn't agreed upon. Instead she'd enjoy the time she had now.

After he kicked the door behind him closed, he lowered her to the floor and pulled her against him, his lips sealing over hers. The moment their mouths met, she no longer had to worry about anything, because her mind went blank and her body took over. Feeling came before thinking.

Although she never wanted the kiss to end, he broke it off and lifted her shirt over her head and tossed it onto the floor. Not wanting to miss out, she grasped for the hem of his tee and did the same thing until she was faced with his tanned, muscular chest. Leaning forward, she pressed her lips against his warm skin, and the big man shuddered, showing her she had power over him. Similar to the power he had over her.

"I want you naked," he said, opening her shorts with a flick of his fingers on the button.

She desired the same thing and shimmied out of her shorts, taking her thong along with them. Next came her bra. Then a shake of each foot and her sandals and clothes were in a pile.

"Your turn," she told him, standing naked before him.

He unhooked the button, slid his hands in the sides, and shed his boxer briefs along with the shorts, also kicking off his shoes.

Before she could take in that naked glorious male body, he picked her up and carried her into a bedroom, depositing her on the bed.

"Now it's time to consummate this marriage." His eyes gleamed with sexual intent.

"For a playboy, you're pretty set on all the traditions of marriage," she informed him.

From the surprise ring to the official proposal to the big wedding and the *something old* he'd made sure she had, if she didn't know better, she'd think he was a true romantic.

He braced his hands on either side of her face, his

body weight pressing against her, his thick erection aligned with her sex. Desire flowed through her, pulsing and heavy.

"Condoms are in the suitcase," he muttered, obviously having no intention of replying to her statement.

He rolled off her and headed for the luggage, returning with more than one packet in hand. He tossed all but one onto the mattress.

He stood by the bed and opened the foil packet, sliding it over his straining shaft before rejoining her on the bed. Kneeling over her, he grabbed on to his cock and slid it back and forth over her sex, being sure to glide over her clit.

Goose bumps prickled over her skin, arousal thrumming inside her. He was sure of himself, and she enjoyed every moment of his ability to make her burn.

She arched her hips, needing him inside her. "Stop teasing me, Jaxon. I want you."

He slid his fingers through her damp folds. "You do. You're so wet for me," he said in a husky voice that revealed how on edge he was.

Positioning himself, he slid the head of his cock inside her and she moaned, reaching for him.

He lowered himself over her, his lips covering hers at the same time he thrust all the way, causing her to see stars. He grasped her hands and lifted her arms above her head and ground his hips into hers, his cock hard and thick inside her.

"Oh, God." She arched her back, bent her knees, and he began to pump his hips, gliding in and out as she squeezed herself around him, causing him to groan and thrust faster, deeper. They were so joined they might as well be a part of each other, and her heart skipped a beat at the thought.

And then he slid his finger over her clit, pressing down as his cock hit the right spot inside her. She cried out and he caught on immediately.

"You like that? I think I should do it again." Raising his hips, he slammed into her again and again and again until she was coming, crying out as he thrust once more and stilled, ending on a low, sexy groan.

*   *   *

JAXON WOKE UP the next morning to Macy's mouth around his hard cock, and before he was even aware of his surroundings, he came hard and fast.

They shared breakfast brought to their room, a continental choice of rolls, muffins, and croissants, their conversation consisting mostly of reminiscing about the wedding and the amazing job Bri had done pulling things together.

Not long after, they were lying on the white sand on a double recliner chair on the beach. Jaxon couldn't tear his gaze from the hot woman beside him in a black-and-white bikini that barely covered her breasts and pussy. If she meant to torture him, she was doing a damn good job. Then again, as he was coming to realize, she didn't have to do more than exist to torture him.

Who'd have thought marital sex would outdo regular sex? After two more rounds before they made it outside, knowing that Macy belonged to him at least for now, their time together had been incredible.

As she lay beside him, he couldn't resist and picked up an ice cube that hadn't yet melted from the bucket and laid it on her belly.

She squealed and popped up from her reclining position. "What are you doing?"

"Cooling you off." He ran the melting cube over her just-tanning skin. "And giving myself something to taste." Leaning over her, he licked the damp driblets on her skin, taking in the salty flavor and groaning as he ran his tongue down to the edge of her bathing suit where heaven waited.

Feeling her eyes on him, he hooked his fingers into the sides of her suit and pulled it down her thighs, revealing her damp sex. She pulled in a shuddering breath as he lowered his head and flicked at her sweet pussy.

She raised her hips and rolled herself against him. It didn't take long for her soft moans to grow until she was coming as he lapped up her juices.

"Good God," she muttered, flopping her body against the chair.

"Glad to be of service." He chuckled, wiping his mouth on his arm and ignoring the hard-on behind his swim trunks.

She shot him a wry look as she slipped her bikini bottoms back up. "Let's go cool off," she said, rose, and started for the ocean.

He followed, completely enthralled with this woman who was now his wife.

They spent the rest of the day alternating between the sun and a cabana, Macy drinking piña coladas and Jaxon his cousin and brother's Dirty Dog Vodka, neat. It was the first truly relaxing day he'd had in ages, and he'd never had such a peaceful time enjoying female company.

She confided in him about how hard it had been growing up having lost her mother, her father's attempt at finding a replacement, and his disappointing ultimate choice of Lilah as his second wife and her stepmother.

They'd already discussed Jesse Prescott that night at dinner with Hannah, so he didn't see the need to bring up the subject today, and apparently neither did she. Which was why, when she did ask him about his family, the subject was a surprise.

"So tell me about Paul being your biological father."

He coughed on his vodka. "It's a weird situation," he admitted. "On the one hand, it was a relief to know Jesse wasn't my dad. That his disappointment in me stemmed more from his feelings about himself, not making pro ball due to an injury. Not being able to have kids. On the other hand, it would have been nice if my mother, knowing the truth, had stepped in."

"I'm not making excuses, but I'm sure she found herself in a tough situation," Macy said.

He nodded. "I know she did. She's admitted as much. My father Jesse's behavior got worse as time went on. She's a good mom, was a buffer when he got to be too verbally abusive. But I have to admit it was a relief when Paul needed a kidney and Mom told us the truth last year."

"Austin was the donor." She shifted on the chair.

He nodded. "I wasn't surprised. I love my brother but he is the golden child. Football player when Dad wanted one, naturally talented, Paul's savior. But he's a great guy. And I would always want him to have my back."

She sighed. "That's how I want Hannah to feel about me one day."

"And she will. You're there for her, you're fighting for her, you do right by her. She's lucky to have you and she'll grow up knowing it. Or come to realize it," he assured her.

She tipped her head to the side, meeting his gaze. "I hope you're right."

He grinned. "I usually am."

She laughed. "Good to know."

She turned her body to her side so they were facing each other. "So I have another question, and you don't have to answer it if you don't want to." She propped her head in her hand, waiting for him to reply.

"We're husband and wife. No secrets, right? Go ahead and ask." Though he wasn't looking forward to the question, he figured they were being open and honest.

"Why don't you believe in marriage? Or at least the happily-ever-after part?"

Once again she'd taken him off guard, but he decided to fill her in. "Well, when I was younger, I did believe." Facing Macy, he forced himself to tell the story. "Katie and I met in college. We got very serious very quickly. She always knew I wanted to play Major League Baseball. And she knew what that entailed. One hundred and sixty-two games a year, excluding postseason, no control in the early days of what state or team I'd end up on. No guarantee of big money, though I was talented."

She laughed at his deliberate tossing in of ego. "Of course you were."

"Anyway, she went into the relationship with eyes wide open. I just don't think she realized my first stop in the minors would be Washington State." His stomach cramped at the reminder of having to deliver the news. He hadn't thought she'd like it, but he had believed they were in it together.

"Pretty far from Florida. I take it that's where she was from?" Macy asked, eyes full of compassion.

"Yes. And suddenly, she couldn't handle the lifestyle. She dumped me very easily considering the plans we'd made."

Reaching out, Macy grasped his hand. "You didn't deserve that."

"Regardless, it did teach me a lesson. Family life isn't for me."

She narrowed her gaze. "I realize you were hurt but don't you think that's shortsighted? It's not like you'll play forever, and a more understanding, stronger woman could most definitely handle being on her own."

She shook her head. "All I'm saying is don't let the rest of your life be defined by something that happened when you were young."

"You sound pragmatic," he said, taking in her words and filing them away to dissect another time.

She shrugged. "I'm just telling it like it is." She squeezed his hand. "We might be short-term but you do deserve happiness."

His stomach twisted at the reminder that this part of his life wasn't permanent, surprising him. He'd only been with Macy for a week, and already he felt a connection with her that was stronger than any he'd experienced before. Even with Katie. And that completely threw him for a loop.

His reaction was to deflect. "How do you feel about lobster?" he asked.

Her eyes danced with the knowledge that he was ending their conversation on purpose. "Love it. Why?"

"Damon can't stop raving about a place he took Evie to when they were here on the island." His brother said it was on the water, romantic, and he highly recommended he bring Macy there. "I made us a dinner reservation tonight if you're up for it."

She smiled. "I am. It sounds great."

"Then it's a date." He rolled onto his back and soaked in the sun, shutting off thoughts of Katie, the past, and losing Macy in the future.

Chapter Ten

MACY RETURNED TO Florida tanned and chilled out, amazed at how one full day on the beach on Sunday and two nights on the island had relaxed her. She also felt closer to her husband and warned herself to be careful and not take his confidences too seriously. They were friends, exchanging information, nothing more. He wasn't trying to win her over or get into her heart. And she didn't want him to. Right? Right.

"Want to pick up Hannah on the way home? We can get started with our family life, picking out her room, winning her over. She has to be upset with Lilah right now, after she canceled their plans," Jaxon suggested.

Macy nodded. "It's a good idea. I miss her. And when I spoke to her from the Bahamas, she sounded hurt." Which wasn't something Macy wanted, but she couldn't deny it helped her in her custody battle.

She *needed* Hannah to want to live with her. "Let's surprise her at Ruby's instead of calling first," she said, excited to pick up her sister.

Jaxon grinned. "Sounds like a plan. Let's do it."

Except when they arrived at Ruby's, Hannah's teenage friend greeted Macy at the door. "Hannah's not here."

"What? Where is she?" Jaxon immediately slid an arm around her shoulder.

"Her mother picked her up this morning with some guy. They left for the day and she took her bag," Ruby said.

Her mother walked up behind her. "I thought it was okay to let her go since Hannah said she was supposed to be with her this weekend before her mom canceled. Is there a problem?" the woman asked, starting to panic.

Jaxon squeezed Macy in warning.

"No. It's fine," she lied, hating that Lilah was playing a game. "Thank you for having her," she said.

"Our pleasure and congratulations on your wedding," Ruby's mom, Cindy, said. "You look tan and happy."

"We are," Jaxon said from behind her, his warm breath on her neck. "I'm sure we'll see Hannah back at the house tonight."

Macy felt certain his words were more for Macy's benefit than conversation with Ruby's mom, and she appreciated his certainty or at least his attempt at reassurance.

She just wasn't sure she believed him.

They walked down the steps and back to the car that was driving them home, sitting in the back seat. "Remember I had both of your things moved to my house this weekend."

She nodded.

"So Hannah couldn't get her own things to go anywhere with her mother. Just stay calm. My hunch tells me she'll show up on my doorstep. That Lilah is just trying to get you to lose your temper."

"Well, I have," she said, clenching and unclenching her fists. "She has no right to make decisions about where Hannah goes. And I should know where my sister is." Her heart pounded in her chest, anger and frustration building.

"We'll talk to Jonathan in the morning. I think it's time to set down some rules via the court. In the meantime, when Hannah gets home, don't give Lilah what she wants. Don't lose it and don't yell at Hannah. Got it?"

She nodded. "I got it. And thank you, because left to my own devices, I would have freaked out."

"We're going to figure this out." He covered his hand with hers.

She dialed Hannah, got her voicemail, and left a message letting her sister know they'd be at Jaxon's, giving her the address, which she already had, but

Macy wasn't taking any chances. She did the same with Lilah, using the number she'd had to force from her sister, who hadn't wanted to share it.

Biting on her lip, she worried about whether Lilah could or would disappear so she'd never see Hannah again and decided against it. Her stepmother needed legal custody for anything she wanted to do with Hannah, from enrolling her in school to taking her out of the country. God forbid.

Deciding Jaxon was right and Lilah was testing her temper, she blew out a breath and glanced at the man keeping her calm.

Turning, she took in his handsome profile, how sexy he looked, how tanned, and she fed off his peaceful mood. She also fed off the sexual tension that hadn't dissipated since they left the island.

He turned his stare from the window and met her gaze, the heat emanating from him a tangible thing. They were married and had an ongoing sexual relationship. She didn't need to pretend she didn't want him. So she slid across the seat, climbed into his lap, and sealed her lips over his.

She kissed him, ignoring the driver in the front seat, pretending they were alone, appreciating the fact that he so easily let her forget her problems. She didn't think Lilah would disappear with Hannah, so what she needed now was to redirect her focus until she saw her sister again.

And Jaxon was the perfect distraction.

With her sex directly over his erection, she began to shift her hips, rocking against him, desire overwhelming her. Taking her to a place where nothing else existed but the sensual feelings flowing through her body.

He slammed his hand down on the seat beside him. "Shut the fucking window," he barked at the driver before gripping her hips and holding her down, his thick cock taking her on a ride of pleasure. Waves built. Need grew. And the partition rose, protecting them from prying eyes though the man clearly knew what was going on in his back seat.

"Keep riding me," Jaxon said in a gruff voice, whispering in her ear.

"Oh, God. It feels so good." The only thing missing was him inside her.

He jerked his hips up, his hard cock rubbing against her clit. She rocked back and forth until she exploded, delicious sensations taking her over into utter bliss. And Jaxon stilled, his low groan telling her he'd come as well. They were like teenagers grabbing time alone in the back seat of a car.

Her cheeks burning when they arrived at his house, she ignored the driver as Jaxon took their bags and led her inside.

They took a quick shower together, Jaxon picking her up and carrying her over his shoulder into the master bath. "After that little performance, you're not leaving me alone."

"I don't want to."

They stripped down and stepped into his gorgeous marble shower with multiple jets, taking turns lathering each other up, her using his woodsy shower soap on him, him using her fruity gel on her. When he said he'd had her things moved, he'd meant everything, and she didn't want to know how he'd accomplished it.

Because they hoped Hannah would show up soon, there was no more playtime in the shower, but he'd promised her the real thing tonight when they climbed into bed.

Her sex gave a pulse of approval at the thought.

* * *

Macy kept calling both Hannah's and Lilah's numbers, neither one of them answering. But that didn't stop her from trying or leaving multiple messages.

Dinner passed. She and Jaxon ordered in Italian food, including Hannah's favorite chicken parmigiana, but she still hadn't come back. They ate in silence though Macy barely tasted her chicken scarpariello.

Not even the hot peppers affected her, she was so

distracted. "If Hannah's not home by eight, I'm calling the police. I have custody and her mother said she couldn't take her this weekend. I didn't give permission for them to be together after Lilah canceled."

"Evie's brother's a detective. I'll text him," Jaxon said, his worried eyes on hers.

She swallowed hard and nodded. "I appreciate it." Just as she placed her fork down, the doorbell rang.

Her eyes met Jaxon's over the table. "Remember, calm, relaxed, don't show your hand. We want Lilah to be shocked when we ask to move up the date of the hearing and request she not be allowed to see Hannah without your permission until then," he reminded her.

Blowing out a breath, she nodded. "I still want to rip Lilah's hair out," she muttered. "I've been worried sick."

She ran for the door and opened it up to find Hannah standing with her bag. Lilah, obviously not wanting an argument, waited in the car.

"Hi, I'm home!" Hannah said, a bright smile on her face.

"So are we. I tried to pick you up at Ruby's." Just because she wasn't going to fight with Lilah didn't mean she wouldn't get the story from her sister.

"Oh! Well, Mom has a boyfriend, and he'd surprised her with show tickets, so she couldn't take me the whole weekend, but she picked me up Sunday morning." Hannah pulled her suitcase in and Macy glanced at Jaxon.

Boyfriend? That was interesting though exactly what Macy had expected. "Did you meet him?" Macy asked Hannah.

Hannah nodded. "He's young," she said, giggling. "And hot. He's a gym manager. I'm hungry. Do you have anything for dinner?" She changed the subject like a pro.

"Hey, kid. We ordered you chicken Parm. I hear it's your favorite. Want to eat or pick your room first?" Jaxon asked her, shaking his head at Macy, obviously warning her to keep her questions light.

"Room! Then food."

Smiling at Hannah's enthusiasm, Macy followed Jaxon and Hannah to the side of the house with three extra bedrooms. It was obvious to Macy that the rooms already had a woman's touch. Probably his mother or Bri had decorated the guest rooms.

"Remember, you can change yours up any way you want," he said.

Hannah ran from room to room.

"Don't go by size," Macy said. "One has a wall across from the bed with the TV, another has a TV on the side. It might be less comfortable watching. One has room for a desk to do your work. Another might not. You and I have time to go through all three and make a decision. Just pick one for tonight," she said.

Hannah chose the one with the bed by the window overlooking the pool. "When can my friends come over?" she asked.

"Maybe next weekend. We'll discuss it." Macy left Hannah in the bedroom to unpack and walked into the hall where Jaxon waited.

"A boyfriend," she said to him, "who's a gym manager. He can't give her the lifestyle she wants." She bit down on the inside of her cheek.

"Add it to the list to give to Jonathan's private investigator and we'll go from there," Jaxon instructed her.

She nodded, a sudden wave of exhaustion overtaking her. But she still had to give her sister dinner and show her where the shower and towels were and discuss a morning schedule for school before turning in for the night.

*   *   *

JAXON MET LINC at the stadium gym, leaving Macy home to work in a sunlit room she'd chosen to use as her work space. They walked inside together because Jaxon had driven them both.

"So will Lizzie and I be seeing you at the Children's Benefit Saturday night?" Linc asked.

"Son of a bitch." He slammed his hand on his

thigh. "I forgot all about it."

Linc chuckled. "Considering all that's going on in your life, I'm not surprised. But it's a mandatory event for all players."

Through the publicity department, the team sponsored an organization that supported kids in foster homes. Meeting and greeting the team in a formal setting encouraged donors to reach deep into their pockets to help the kids, and even if it hadn't been required, Jaxon wouldn't have missed it.

But all *he* needed to do was put on a tuxedo, which he had hanging in his closet, cleaned, pressed, and ready to go.

"Which means I have to spring a formal event on Macy." He knew from having a sister that women liked to buy new dresses for big nights out. "Wonderful," he muttered, and then an idea came to him. He paused outside the locker room and dialed his sister.

"Good news only," Brianne answered.

"Then I guess it depends on your mood. I have a black-tie event Saturday night that I forgot about. I have to tell Macy and she'll need a dress. Didn't you once tell me you have a personal shopper somewhere?"

"Yes," she said with an overly dramatic sigh.

"Can you have her pull things and send them over to the house? Or better yet bring them over herself with shoes and accessories?"

Beside him, Linc coughed.

"Shut up," Jaxon muttered. "You'd do the same thing if the situation were reversed."

Linc turned his head to the side. "Because I'm in love with Lizzie. What's your excuse?"

Bri burst out laughing. "He's got you there, little brother. Okay, I'm on it, but I'm sure it's going to cost you big bucks being so last-minute."

"It's fine. Thanks for handling it. I'll call you later."

He disconnected and ignored Linc's smirk as he called Macy to let her know she had to dress up for the role of baseball player's wife.

*   *   *

FOR HER OFFICE, Macy had taken over a room on the lower level of Jaxon's house with a set of windows overlooking his beautiful property. The custody hearing loomed in the distance, but so far, Lilah had been behaving, calling Hannah on her cell, asking Macy before picking her up from school once during the early part of the week. Not wanting to rock things, Macy hadn't asked her lawyer to move anything up. She wasn't ready for a court date. Instead she put her nerves aside and tried to live her life. Which, at the moment, meant work.

With Hannah at school and Jaxon at the gym, her

muse flowed in her new surroundings and work came easily, even the back-end coding.

When her cell phone rang, it startled her out of a deep trance. She saw Jaxon's name and answered immediately. "Hi, Jaxon. Everything okay?"

"Fine. I just…"

"Spit it out," she heard Linc say, laughing.

"I guess there's no good way to tell you. I forgot about a mandatory black-tie team fundraising event Saturday night that we both need to attend."

She groaned. "I don't have anything to wear for a formal event." She paused. "Although I could wear the white dress from Damon's wedding, but it's not floor-length," she said, not liking the idea.

"I've got you covered. Bri and a personal stylist will be over with dresses this afternoon."

"Oh!" His words shocked her. "You didn't have to do that but wow. Okay. That's amazing. I know what those baseball wives are going to look like, and I want to keep up," she said, he figured more to herself than to him. "Jaxon, thank you!"

She disconnected the call and was about to dial Bri to find out what time she'd be over when her doorbell rang. She answered it and found her friend standing on the step. "Surprise!"

She grinned. "I just got off the phone with Jaxon. I hear we have dresses coming."

"We do." Bri walked into the house and Macy shut the door. "And you should know this was all his idea. Not mine."

A warm feeling flowed through her at the knowledge. He could have handed her money and told her to go buy a dress. Instead he'd taken care of the situation himself. "This was generous of him," she murmured. "And I'm grateful because I don't have a formal gown."

Bri put an arm around her shoulder. "In about an hour, you will."

Sure enough, in sixty minutes, the doorbell rang and a young woman named Ari Zanders strode in. Behind her was a man rolling a rack of clothing, long gowns with sequins and other decorative items adorning the dresses.

A jolt of excitement rippled through her. Call her shallow, but she was a woman excited by the opportunity to dress up in fancy clothes and pick her favorite.

They hijacked the master bedroom, and for the next forty-five minutes, she pivoted, twirled, and spun as she tried on each piece, finally settling on a gold dress that wrapped around her body as if it were made for her. A strip of sheer material covered her stomach in a classy way.

"This is it!"

Bri clapped slowly. "I agree."

"So do I," Ari said, then called for the man in the truck to take the other dresses back to the store. Ari had come in her own car. Then she helped pin the bottom of the dress for tailoring, promising it would be delivered by Friday so Macy would have it for the event on Saturday night.

"I can't thank you enough," Macy said, her hands clasped together.

"It was my pleasure," Ari said.

Macy glanced in the mirror once more. "I just love it." She held her hair up, debating if she wanted a sophisticated bun or long ringlets falling over her shoulders.

An impressed whistle sounded, and when she turned, Jaxon leaned against the doorframe, his hot gaze settled on hers. "Spectacular," he said in a gruff voice he used when she affected him on a sexual level.

"Told you I'd handle it," Bri said, grinning at her brother. She picked up her handbag. "I've got to get going. Call me," she said to Macy.

"I will. And thank you."

She winked. "Any time for you."

Jaxon, still leaning on the doorframe, watched Bri gather the rest of her things. "I know you love me, sis."

"I have to. You're my brother." Having had the

last word, she started for the door and Macy chuckled.

"You two," she said with a shake of her head. "It must be nice to have a big family." She had Hannah, of course, but until she grew up, their relationship would be more like parent-child.

Jaxon let out a low laugh. "It has its moments."

"If you just take off the dress, I'll take it to the seamstress," Ari said, gathering her things.

"Yes, Macy. Take off the dress." Jaxon's sexy gruff voice caused her nipples to pucker beneath the fabric and her cheeks to flame.

"Oh, my." Ari also blushed and fanned her face.

"And I'm out," Bri said and swept past her brother, taking her exit.

Macy narrowed her gaze at Jaxon.

The sexual undercurrents were vibrant and unmistakable and should be confined to the two of them alone. She ducked into the bathroom and changed out of the gown and into the lightweight dress she'd left there, returning to hand Ari the garment she'd draped over her arm.

As Macy wrapped things up with Ari, she felt the heat of Jaxon's stare, and it was all she could do to say goodbye to the woman without a tremble in her voice, but she managed.

"Alone at last."

She met his dark indigo gaze. "Don't get excited.

Hannah's going to be home soon."

"Then we'll have to be quick." He stepped closer and her heart hammered harder in her chest.

The man always had this effect on her. If he was near, she desired him. Wearing a pair of sweats and a tee he'd changed into after working out, his hair damp from the shower, he smelled clean and manly, the musky scent adding to her arousal.

She glanced at her Apple watch. "Really quick."

A devilish gleam filled his eyes. "Not a problem."

Before she could process his intent, he lifted her dress, pulled it over her head, and tossed it to the floor, leaving her in her thong and nothing else. Because she'd been home alone working, she hadn't even put on a bra. He then slid the thin scrap of material down her legs and waited for her to step out of it before piling it on top of her dress.

"Remember I have to leave to pick up Hannah soon."

"You'll make it there on time," he said, kneeling down.

"What—"

He shut her up by grasping her thighs, spreading her legs, then, dipping his head, he began to pleasure her. He lapped at her with his tongue, sliding along the seam of her sex, causing ripples of desire to cascade through her.

She braced her hands on his shoulders and arched her hips forward, giving him further access. His strong hands held her up as he devoured her, sucking her clit into his mouth and pulling on the tender bud. Sensation, the beginning of a long, slow climax took hold. Her legs shook and she moved her hands from his shoulders to his hair, tugging harder the higher she soared.

He lapped and nipped, and suddenly she came hard, waves of intense pleasure filling her until she moaned loudly. "Jaxon, oh, God, so good." She ground her sex against his mouth, milking every last amazing feeling before her knees gave out on her.

He held on to her as she fell and ended up lying against him. "Like I said, fast and quick."

"And pretty spectacular. But we don't have time for me to take care of you," she said, her gaze on the large bulge behind his sweats.

"I'll be fine. I'll use the twenty-minute trip to the school to cool off." He helped her to her feet, pressed a kiss to her lips, and damned if her nipples didn't pucker once more.

"I was going to get Hannah."

He shook his head. "I don't mind. You go shower." He winked at her and strode out of the room, leaving her body buzzing and her head spinning.

The man's impact was potent, and sex aside, which

was phenomenal, the fact that he'd taken the stress off finding a dress labeled him as special, at least to her.

*   *   *

THE NIGHT BEFORE the charity event, after Hannah had gone to sleep, Jaxon and Macy climbed into bed at the same time.

"It's starting to feel more natural," he said.

"What is?" she asked.

"This. Us."

She settled into the bed and nodded. Without him asking, she slid over to his side of the bed and he pulled her into him. "Yeah. It does feel more natural."

The first few nights of sharing his bed had been awkward as they found their way to being comfortable with each other. But they'd woken up, bodies entwined, the moment always culminating in sex, once or twice from behind as he'd entered her slick wetness, pumped his hips, and she'd begun to come immediately. They were always in sync. And after an intense conversation and exchanged recent blood test results, they had given up condoms.

But every time they met on opposite sides of the bed, it felt like they were starting all over again. Until tonight. She was more relaxed and so was he. As if this afternoon's tryst in the bedroom had broken down that final wall of acceptance of their situation. For them both.

"Are you nervous about meeting the guys and their wives and girlfriends tomorrow night?" he asked, knowing the sports wife was a different breed. High-end handbags, shoes, makeup always done perfectly. It was why he'd made sure Macy would have the outer trappings, to be sure she'd feel like she fit in.

"Not really. I can handle myself."

"You certainly can. And I'll be there for backup."

She shifted and turned to face him. "Have you brought many dates with you to these events?"

Her question surprised him. "Actually, no."

She rose and sat cross-legged, looking adorably sexy in a pale blue camisole top and her barely there panties, and asked, "Why not?"

"Because I never wanted to send the wrong impression."

"And what would that be?" she asked.

"That I wanted a relationship."

She rocked back and forth and asked, "Because of what happened with Katie?"

He wasn't surprised she'd asked the question. He'd already confided in her about his past and how much that relationship had meant to him. "Yeah. I thought it was better that any woman knew going in what she could or couldn't expect. And I also discovered that what you imply is just as important as what you state.

So no women came with me to team events. Until you."

"Did you ever consider the fact that Katie was young, too? That the thought of being alone so often in an unfamiliar state so far from family was frightening? She hadn't had the chance to know who she was as a person yet. To define herself or a career or know what she could do to develop her own life apart from you?"

He let that notion float around in his mind before answering. "To be honest, no. Because after we broke up, I shut off the part of me that considered love and relationships, and I certainly didn't spend any time delving into why Katie did what she did."

"Hmm." Macy folded her arms across her chest, and he'd be lying if he said his gaze wasn't drawn to the cleavage that pushed up as a result.

"Hmm what?"

"Just that by refusing to look back at what happened with Katie, you might miss out on a very different future than the one you imagine."

"Are we finished discussing this?" he asked. Because he really didn't want to think about another woman while he was in bed with his wife.

Wife.

With Macy, that word didn't sound so bad. But despite her nudging him to dissect the reasons Katie had called things off with him, the fact remained, he had a hard time believing a woman wouldn't grow tired of the life he lived.

And he wasn't giving up pitching until he had to.

Chapter Eleven

A s MACY WALKED toward him in the house, she looked like a goddess in her gown and heels, her makeup done by a professional Bri had called to come to the house. Glam Squad, she'd called it and laughed as she'd informed him she'd just tack it onto his Dare Nation bill.

Hannah had a friend over, and the girls had been made up by the cosmetician for fun. Their excitement had been contagious. Prior to them leaving the house, Hannah had pulled out her cell phone camera and insisted on taking pictures of Jaxon and Macy all dressed up. A funny feeling twisted his stomach as he'd wrapped an arm around Macy's waist and smiled for the photo, as if they were a real couple, document-ing their lives for posterity. The future.

And when Hannah's friend insisted on taking a picture of the three of them together, that family feeling had increased. Everything he experienced with Macy was fresh and new, and he couldn't say he disliked the change.

Now, as Jaxon entered the museum where tonight's gala was being held, he was proud to have Macy beside him. He introduced Macy to his teammates, their wives, and significant others, and she charmed everyone she met with an easy smile and a way of making small talk that kept everyone at ease.

Linc and his wife, Lizzie, made their way over. Since they'd been at the wedding, Jaxon didn't need to make introductions. "Hello, you two," he said.

"Hi, Jaxon. Macy." Linc smiled and hugged Macy while Jaxon did the same with Lizzie, then the women said their hellos.

"What table are you at?" Lizzie, a petite yet voluptuous redhead, asked. With so many team members here, they had a large number of tables where the players were spread out.

"Five. You?" Macy asked.

"Five, too. Excellent! We can talk more there," Lizzie said. "I've been meaning to call you to go out for coffee, but time's gotten away from me. Work has been busy."

"You're a real estate agent, right?" Macy asked.

Lizzie nodded.

"Perfect! I'm thinking about selling my house. Or should I say my father's old house."

She was? Jaxon frowned, as she hadn't mentioned a word. Of course, it made sense. Why pay property taxes, electric, and other things on a place she didn't need while she was living with him? But where would she go after they were divorced? Only married a week and his stomach cramped at the notion of not seeing her every day.

"Maybe we could do that coffee, and I'll do a walk-through on the same day," Lizzie said.

"Sounds perfect." Macy smiled and he was drawn to the gorgeous way she looked in the gold gown. She'd disappeared for an hour today and returned with a spray tan that made her skin glow.

Linc appeared to scan the room, then spoke. "Oh, I see Garner. I need to have a word with him. See you at the table?"

Jaxon nodded and waited for Lizzie to follow her husband to their next couple before turning toward Macy. "I didn't know you were considering selling the house."

She glanced up at him, her big brown eyes done up with shadow and liner, her lashes thick and full. "Living in your house made me realize it was past time for me to move out of my father's house and buy a place of my own when the time comes. Now that Hannah's made the break from her routine, it'll be easier to deal with her emotions then. Besides, we don't know when that will be. It could be a year or two or six months. I just want to be prepared."

Her words made sense, but he wished she'd told

him so they could discuss it together. Which meant he was thinking more like a real couple than two people sharing a house and a bed.

First he'd been worried about missing her when she was gone, now he was wanting a more genuine relationship. Shit, he was a mess, and he deepened his frown at his thoughts.

"I'm going to the ladies' room," Macy said, oblivious to his emotional confusion. "I'll find you when I get back."

He nodded and headed to the bar for a glass of Scotch. After he ordered and picked up the glass from the dark wood bar, he took one step and ran into his brothers.

"Austin!" He'd expected Dare Nation to have a presence here. "Braden? What are you doing here?" he asked his sibling who, though he'd shaved enough to show up with only some scruff tonight, he also appeared uncomfortable in the monkey suit they were all required to wear.

Guilt swamped him. Ever since Braden had returned, Jaxon had been busy with his wedding, honeymoon, and new life. He should have reached out to see how his sibling was doing and resolved to do better.

Austin placed a hand on their sibling's shoulder. "I'm introducing the doctor around. If he's going to stay home, he's going to need a job."

Jaxon raised a brow. "You're staying in Florida?"

"Considering it," Braden said.

"But if he's offered a job, then he'll be motivated to stick around. So here we are."

Braden shot Austin a wry smile. "He's always trying to run the show."

"You can say that again," Jaxon muttered.

"So where's your beautiful wife?" Braden asked, taking a sip of the drink in his hand.

"Ladies' room. She should be back any minute."

As they continued to talk, he kept an eye out, and when he caught sight of her, her glow and easy smile were gone.

As soon as she joined them, he asked, "What's wrong?"

She met his gaze. "I'm so sorry."

"What? For what?"

Her knuckles turned white as she gripped her handbag. "Hannah had a party at your house that got out of hand. Someone called the press."

Austin groaned. "More press. The very thing we were trying to avoid."

"Oh, God." Macy's shoulders sagged in defeat.

With a glare at his brother, Jaxon wrapped an arm around Macy's shoulder. "Let me go explain what happened to my manager. He's got teenagers. He'll understand." He used that opportunity to shoot daggers at Austin again for making Macy feel guiltier than she already did. "Then we'll get home and handle things."

"I'll call Bri," Austin said, pulling out his phone from his breast pocket.

Jaxon shook his head. "No. Not until I have a handle on what happened. And if she calls you, tell her to sit tight until she hears from me." He slid his hand down and clasped palms with Macy. "I want to know what happened, and her sister's privacy comes first. Do you understand?"

He was telling Austin to put Macy and her sister first before protecting his own reputation. In no time, these two women had come to mean something to him, and he would safeguard them, even at his expense.

Austin met his gaze, his own expression as serious as Jaxon had ever seen it. "I understand. I just hope you do."

Jaxon did. He cared about Macy and Hannah, and it scared the living shit out of him. But he turned his focus to Macy. "Let's go make our excuses and get out of here."

She squeezed his hand in reply and what he sensed was gratitude. What she didn't understand was that he knew what it was like to be a team. And he was coming to feel like they were one.

*   *   *

MACY WANTED TO throw up. She'd married Jaxon not just to help retain custody of her sister but to keep him out of the press. They'd left Hannah alone for the first time at Jaxon's house, and she'd gone and had a party that could destroy his career. Yes, his manager had been understanding, but she'd seen the look on the team owner's face at the word *viral*. The man was pissed, and Jaxon was going to take the brunt of her sister's actions.

She didn't speak on the way home, her fury at her sister simmering inside her. Jaxon merely held on to her hand and his temper. He hadn't once launched into a tirade over Hannah's behavior, while she was ready to throttle her sister.

And when they pulled into the driveaway and saw Lilah's car, Macy's anger skyrocketed. "What is she doing here?" She unhooked her seat belt and grabbed the door handle.

"Wait." Jaxon grasped her wrist. "We need a plan. And it starts with staying calm and finding out what happened before you go off on her."

She expelled a long breath. She turned to face Jaxon, who'd unhooked his bow tie and opened the top of his dress shirt. Even disheveled, his hair messed from running his hand through it and his suit undone, he was handsome and sexy. He was also much more relaxed than her.

They'd had to leave the party early. Their seats would be noticeably empty. Another strike against him, and it was her sister's fault.

"I'm so sorry." She shook her head. "I shouldn't have left Hannah alone."

A wry smile lifted his lips. "She's fifteen. My mother left us alone at that age. Sometimes we behaved and sometimes we didn't."

She nodded, grateful for his understanding. "We might as well go see what we're dealing with."

The fact that there were no cops at the house calmed her somewhat. Media was one thing. Legal troubles another.

He pulled the car, the Lamborghini she'd learned he saved for special occasions, into the garage, and together they met by the door to the house.

As he grasped her hand, they stepped inside and walked through the hall and into the family room. Red cups were spread all over, while Lilah and Hannah were rushing around, cleaning up, dumping the plastic into the trash, and setting the turned-over tchotchkes to their former upright positions.

"I'd like an explanation," Macy said, startling them both.

Hannah, red cups in each hand, turned to face her. Her cheeks were flushed, her eyes red from crying. "I didn't mean for this to happen, I swear. I invited a few friends over. Actually two. Okay four. But two of them thought it would be cool to announce a party at Jaxon Prescott's house on their pages."

She spoke fast, obviously trying to get all the information out at once. "And the next thing I knew, people were pouring into the house. I was freaking out the whole time, I swear. I tried to clean up as things went along, but everything got out of hand." She tossed the cups from her hand into a large green garbage bag and started to cry.

Before Macy could get to her, Lilah stepped over and wrapped an arm around her daughter. "When things got out of control, Hannah called her mother. Because she knows she can trust me. I came over to help her clean up the mess the kids left." She looked around the room before settling her gaze on Macy. "And it's a good thing I did, because the police showed up soon after, and they had to ask permission to come inside. I said no. So they gave me a warning to get the kids out of the house and not to have an underage party again." She wiped her hands as if she'd handled the problem to everyone's satisfaction.

Which she seemed to have done. But it didn't make sense that Lilah knew she could refuse to let the police enter. Macy hadn't known that. In fact, faced with a police officer, she'd probably do whatever they asked. This situation aside, Macy just didn't trust Lilah.

Macy narrowed her gaze. "You're saying that you looked out for us."

Lilah shook her head. "I looked out for Hannah and, by extension, both of you. The only way police can constitutionally enter a house are with a warrant, consent, or exigent circumstances. I denied consent," she said, sounding proud of herself.

How did Lilah know these things? Macy tucked the question away for a later time. Lilah's actions didn't help Jaxon with his team, but they did prevent a bigger scandal and problems with the law, all of which begged the question, *why*? She could have gained even more of a custodial upper hand by letting the police inside.

"I suppose I should say thank you?" Macy asked.

"Not so fast." Jaxon glanced at Hannah. "You, Macy, and I will talk later, but can you give the three of us a few minutes?" He tipped his head toward the bedrooms, indicating Hannah should go to her room.

"Umm, yeah." She took the opportunity to leave and quickly darted out.

Confused and curious, Macy glanced at Jaxon. "What's going on?"

He looked at Lilah, the picture of innocence in a

pair of jeans and a loose, flowing top, casual without makeup, like her daughter had called her and she'd rushed out to help her.

"How did the police know to come by? We have no neighbors the kids' noise would be bothering." He owned such a large parcel of land, they couldn't see his neighbors, Macy realized.

"And better yet, how did the paparazzi know there was a party at my house? Because I doubt they were following social media pages of kids in high school." Jaxon pinned her with a knowing glare.

Although there was a damned good chance the paps were hanging out by his house, waiting for something like the morning she'd left doing the walk of shame, Macy assumed this was Jaxon's way of pushing Lilah into an admission.

"I'm sure the paparazzi follow police scanners," Lilah said, not meeting Jaxon's gaze.

And the wheels in Macy's head began to turn. About Lilah and how she could use this situation to her advantage yet still look like the more caring parent.

"Hannah called you because you're the good friend in her eyes, not a parent teaching her right from wrong," Macy said, laying things out. "You helped her clean up and sweep away her problem, and now she's grateful to you. Maybe she even wants to live with you." Her stomach churned at that thought and reminder that her sister had once said that she preferred Lilah to Macy.

"Of course I did those things. I want to do whatever I can for my daughter."

Jaxon folded his arms across his chest. "And after she called, I'll bet you did a quick Google search. Looked up the law on open house parties. After which you called the cops, probably anonymously," he said. "And then you called the paparazzi. So now Macy and I look bad. Less fit guardians than you. And if you think I can't hire the right people to find out if you made those calls, think again."

The satisfied gleam in Lilah's gaze was all Macy needed. "You bitch." Macy started toward her, but Jaxon grabbed before she could lunge at the other woman. Not that Macy knew what she'd have done. Just that the anger and hurt flowing through her were out of control.

She drew a deep breath and calmed herself down. "Get out. Until our court hearing next week, don't ask to see Hannah. The answer is no."

"Come. I'll walk you out." Striding over, Jaxon took Lilah's elbow, and she immediately shook him off.

Macy lowered herself onto the sofa, leaned back against the cushions, and groaned, waiting for Jaxon to return, hearing Lilah's complaints and threats as he escorted her to the door.

A few seconds later, he returned to the room. "She's gone," he said softly, walking to where she sat and settled in beside her.

"I'm sorry," she said again and he shook his head.

"Stop. There's no reason to apologize. Hannah is a teenager and this is pretty normal behavior as far as that goes."

She slid her fingers over the material on her thighs in a nervous movement. "I saw the look on the team owner's face. He's furious, Jaxon. I just gave you more bad press instead of less."

"And I saw my manager's understanding. He'll smooth things over. Seriously. I can handle this. I'm more worried about how it'll look for you at the custody hearing."

Macy glanced at him, tears in her eyes. "Not good. Hannah's given Lilah very solid ammunition to use against us. Not that I think she'd be a better parent, but I know she's a stellar actress."

"Come here." He pulled her against him, and Macy snuggled in, resting her head on his shoulder. "I have to punish Hannah. She can't have a party and get away with it."

"She said she didn't intend for it to be a party," Jaxon reminded her.

Macy inhaled, breathing in his masculine scent, and

snuggled in closer, needing him. "Then she should have called me and been honest instead of calling her mother, hoping to cover up the evidence. Hannah didn't know Lilah would turn this into a shit show. She thought she'd help her clean up and pretend the party never happened."

He groaned. "You're right. There should be consequences," he reluctantly agreed. "Since you've already prohibited Lilah from seeing Hannah, why don't you use that as her punishment. It's pretty light considering what she did."

"You can't keep me from my mother!" Hannah shouted, walking in from the hallway.

Macy's head began to pound as she pushed herself up from her seat. "Come on, Hannah. You had to know there would be punishment."

"Not if I lived with Mom!" she yelled back, hysterical.

"Your mother is putting on an act. Showing you what you want to see. It wouldn't be the same if you lived with her, trust me."

"You're just jealous that I have a mother." And with that shot, Hannah ran for her room and slammed the door.

"She didn't mean that." Jaxon rose and wrapped his arms around her, pulling her against him.

"For the moment she did." And it had been like an

arrow to her heart. "And when I make her clean up the rest of this room, she'll have some other choice words for me."

"Part of parenting, or so I'm learning," he said with a chuckle.

"Regretting our marriage?" she asked into his chest, not wanting to see his face.

He waited a beat before answering. "Not for a minute."

At his words, tears that had filled her eyes fell and dampened his shirt. He was so easy to like and would be even easier to love. If only he could trust her not to hurt him the way his ex-fiancée had. But he'd been clear about his intentions going into this marriage and with women in general. She wouldn't push or hope for more than he was willing or capable of giving.

She stepped back, glanced at his shirt, and winced. "There's makeup all over you."

"That's what dry cleaners are for. Come on. Let's get to sleep. Things will look better in the morning."

As he wrapped an arm around her shoulder and headed for the bedroom, she hoped he was right.

*   *   *

JAXON WOKE UP first. He knew how long it had taken Macy to fall asleep, and she'd tossed and turned for hours. He wasn't sure which part of last night upset her more. The party and Hannah's betrayal, calling her mother and not Macy when things got out of hand, or that Jaxon might take the brunt of the information that had gone viral. Probably all of it.

He wasn't thrilled, and the end result definitely was contrary to the reason they'd gotten married in the first place—lying low, staying under the radar, chilling out by having a family. But Jaxon did think his coach, having teenagers himself, understood. The owner? Coach would smooth things over or Jaxon trusted Austin to call and talk to him today. Jaxon definitely didn't blame Macy. He'd had plenty of parties behind his parents' backs when he was a kid.

He glanced at her asleep beside him and felt a sense of peace. The feeling was as foreign to him as the calmness he experienced having both Macy and Hannah in his home, prior to last night's antics. The three of them eating a rushed breakfast before school, the hum of music from the room that was now Macy's office, someone to come home to after working out, it was all better than he'd anticipated.

He studied her profile and admitted to himself that he was falling in love with her. Everything about their relationship had been rushed, but because of Macy's honest personality and how deeply she drew him in, the feelings were genuine.

Panic set in as he realized he didn't know if he was

alone in his emotions, and he knew how difficult it was to trust another woman with his heart. Even Macy. He pulled her into his arms and she didn't wake up. He used the time to stay calm and remember Macy's comments about how youth might have colored both his emotions and Katie's reactions. He was an adult now, he and Macy were married, and he had time to build a foundation with her before admitting his growing feelings.

The thought relaxed him and he must have fallen back to sleep, because the next thing he knew, Macy was standing by the bed, shaking him awake.

"What's wrong?" He pushed himself to a sitting position.

"Hannah's not in her room. She's not in the house and she's not taking my calls." She ran a hand through her hair, messing it up as she continued to work herself into a frenzy.

He narrowed his gaze. "I set the alarm before we went to bed." And he'd given both Macy and Hannah the code in case they came home without him or needed to leave. "We would have heard the beeps if she unset it."

"Well, she did unset it and neither one of us woke up!"

He rubbed his hand over his face, still exhausted. Last night had probably made them crash hard. "It's pretty easy to guess where she went. Did you call Lilah?"

Macy shook her head. "I was too busy panicking. Damn that credit card I gave her for emergencies. She probably took an Uber." She turned over the phone in her hand and pulled up Lilah's name, then hit send.

"Lilah, is Hannah with you?" Macy asked.

Jaxon watched her pace, her tanned legs peeking out from the edge of the long tee shirt she wore.

"Well, can I speak to her?" As she listened, Macy's eyes opened wide. "I don't care what she's busy doing, put her on the phone." She paused, then said, "Never mind. Just tell her I'm coming to get her and she'd better be downstairs in the lobby and waiting."

He wondered what Lilah's reply would be, and then Macy spoke again. "You might be her mother, but I have custody and she walked out of here without permission. So have her ready when I get there unless you want me coming with the police."

Silence and then, "Fine. No later than two." She stabbed at her phone with her finger, ending the call. "Ugh. That woman is going to make me crazy, and as for my sister, Lilah said Hannah's upset and she'll bring her back this afternoon. I let it go."

He patted the bed and she sat down. He slid over and began to massage her shoulders, working on the knots he found there.

Leaning forward, he whispered, "Relax. At least you know Hannah is safe." He kissed the skin behind her ear and watched as she shivered, goose bumps prickling on her skin. "And now we have time alone, so why don't we make the most of it?"

He felt the moment her muscles eased up and she let herself fall into the moment. Her head tipped, her hair fell forward, revealing the back of her neck, and he took advantage, running his lips over her flesh. He slipped his hands around her waist, beneath her shirt, and cupped her bare breasts.

"Mmm. You know how to make me forget my troubles."

He chuckled, low and deep. "I aim to please," he said, tweaking her nipples between his thumbs and forefingers.

She squirmed at the sensation; meanwhile his cock jerked in his boxer briefs, hard and ready for more than a slow and sensual perusal of her body. But he took his time, wanting to tease and play with her a bit before he slid inside her. Clearly she had other plans, because she turned and pushed him down onto the mattress before straddling him.

Her hands on his shoulders, she bent down and kissed him, her lips soft on his, her damp sex grinding against his straining dick. Then she rose and lifted her shirt over her head, tossing it aside, giving him a view of her breasts, her nipples red from his fingers, causing him to groan.

He hooked his fingers into her lace underwear and pulled on the thin fabric. Taking the hint, she slid off him and removed her panties while he maneuvered his boxer briefs off as well. She positioned herself, her knees on either side of his waist, and rose, a goddess with her hair hanging over her shoulders.

She grasped his cock and settled him into her, sliding down until their bodies were one. He groaned at the feel of her, tight and slick around him, and she began to glide up and down, riding him, taking control until their eyes met and sensation gave way to something more.

And in that moment, he knew. He wasn't falling in love. He had already fallen. He was in too deep to escape and didn't know what to do. Then she squeezed her inner walls and he groaned, lifting his hips, their bodies meeting again and again until she came, her hips rocking, her entire body spasming around him. Her climax triggered his own, and he slammed his hips upward and ground into her.

A few minutes later, she lay splayed across him, breathing heavily. "I needed that." She rolled to the side, flipping her hair off her face.

"Any time." He grinned, taking in the flush in her cheeks. "How about you shower and I'll check in with

Jonathan. See if he's got any leverage on Lilah," he said of the lawyer they'd hired.

She played with his hair, her gaze soft on his. "Are you sure you don't want to shower with me and we can call Jonathan after?" she asked in a tempting voice.

And he was tempted. But with his heart on the line and her feelings unknown, he needed distance. "I need to call Austin, too."

"Okay. Let me know what they say." She kissed him on the lips and rolled out of bed, leaving him alone.

Chapter Twelve

MACY SHOWERED, LETTING the warm water run over her skin, soaping her body with strawberry gel, replacing Jaxon's masculine scent with the fruity one. She didn't kid herself. She couldn't rid herself of Jaxon if she wanted to and she didn't. She loved him. But he had so many walls built up around him she didn't know if she'd ever get through.

They'd had a moment in bed earlier. She shampooed her hair and tipped her head back to let the bubbles run off. Their bodies had been connected, and for a moment, she'd thought their hearts had as well. But afterwards, she'd felt his defenses go back up and knew he was shutting her out.

Oh, he'd be there for her with Hannah, help deal with the lawyer, go up against Lilah. But the glimpse she'd gotten of his heart? That was locked up tight again.

After conditioning her hair and rinsing off, she stepped out of the shower and onto the fluffy bathroom mat. She dried off and pulled on a dress she'd taken into the bathroom with her and wrapped her damp hair in a bun to dry.

She headed to the kitchen, where she found Jaxon standing by the granite counter, drinking a cup of coffee. "Hi."

"Hi. Coffee?" He gestured to the brewer.

"I can make it, thanks. Any news from Jonathan?"

He stepped aside so she could get to the machine, and while she popped in a K-cup, he filled her in. "Nothing worth mentioning about Lilah except a low bank balance—don't ask how he knows that because I didn't—and a boyfriend who doesn't have much more money than she does."

"You'd think that Hannah is wealthy and that's why she wants custody but—" She was about to explain how Hannah's insurance from their father was tied up in trust with Macy as trustee and that money was set aside for college when Hannah's voice sounded through the house followed by the front door slamming.

"Oh, shit." Macy put the mug down before even taking a sip and rushed to meet her sister in the hall.

Given the black streaks of tears running down Hannah's face, Macy opted not to lay into her now for sneaking out without leaving a note or asking permission.

"I hate her!"

Macy met Jaxon's gaze. He appeared as shocked as

Macy was. "Who do you hate?" she asked, just to be clear.

"Mom. I overheard her talking to her boyfriend. Do you want to know why she wants me? Because Dad left me insurance and getting custody would give her control of the money." Her eyes filled again. "He said I was baggage she had to take to get the money but it would be worth it."

That bitch. Macy was going to kill her. She pulled Hannah into a hug. "Honey, I'm so sorry your mother disappointed you."

Hannah sniffed. "I wanted to live with her because she was fun. She never got mad at me. She didn't make me do anything like clean up. I thought it meant she loved me more than you did."

Jaxon arrived with tissues in his hand and gave them to Hannah, then discreetly stepped away.

"Hannah, I love you. I've always told you that. And all the arguments and punishments, those are because I want what's best for you. And that's for you to grow up to be a woman with morals and a good sense of right and wrong."

"I'm sorry." Hannah wiped her face with the tissues, the black mascara smearing even more. Suddenly her eyes opened wide. "What if Mom gets custody of me? She made me sign a piece of paper saying I wanted to live with her, but that was before. What am

I going to do?" She began to panic, wring her hands, and pace.

"Hannah, stop and listen to me. Your money is in a trust. I'm in charge, and even if your mother got custody, she couldn't touch the money." Which meant Lilah wasn't going to want her daughter, and Macy didn't want to be the one to give Hannah the cold facts.

She wrapped an arm around her sister's shoulder. "You should go up and wash your face and shower. We can talk about everything that happened some more, and you leaving this house without permission, later."

Hannah sniffed and nodded. "What are you going to do?" she asked, because she knew Macy well.

"Jaxon and I are going to talk and decide whether I should go lay out the facts for your mom or let the lawyer do it for me." Although Macy wanted to confront Lilah and see her face when she realized the money her dad had left was protected from her greedy hands. "What's Lilah's hotel room number?" she asked.

Hannah mumbled the answer, and once she'd disappeared and Macy heard the door to the bedroom close, Jaxon returned from wherever he'd disappeared to.

"I didn't want to embarrass her by being here

when she was crying. Or admitting her mother didn't really want her." He shook his head. "Poor kid."

Macy frowned. "Better she learn the truth now than after some judge awarded custody to Lilah because she was the biological mother." Her stomach cramped at the thought of how easily that result could have occurred.

"I want to confront her myself," Macy said. "Is it awful that I want to see her reaction?" She shook her head. "All of this upheaval because she somehow found out about Dad's insurance. I'm sure they spoke about it when they were married. Dad was really good about estate planning. Lilah just obviously isn't very smart about how it works."

Jaxon folded his arms across his chest, a move she always loved because it displayed his muscular forearms.

"How about I stay with the kid. I can distract her when she comes down, and you can go have it out with your stepmother," he suggested.

"Perfect. Thank you." She walked over, rose to her tiptoes, and pressed a kiss to his cheek. She was grateful and wanted him to know it. "Hold down the fort," she said with a wink before heading to get her purse and car keys.

She had a confrontation to get to and a woman to get out of her sister's life for good.

*　　*　　*

MACY'S ANGER HAD time to fester on the drive to the hotel where Lilah was staying. She left the car with the valet, strode through the luxurious mirrored lobby, and took the elevator to the eighth floor.

After following the signs, she banged on the door number Hannah had given her and waited. When no one answered, she raised her hand to knock harder, but the door flung open and Lilah greeted her.

"Good job. You all but destroyed your daughter. Are you happy?" Macy pushed her way inside, intending to have the argument in private.

"Excuse me!"

"We need to talk and I'm not doing it in the hallway." Macy waited until Lilah shut the door before speaking. "Are we alone or is your boyfriend here?" She wanted to know what she was dealing with.

"We're alone. Is Hannah okay? I've been calling her to make sure she got home safely but she won't answer."

Macy studied her and realized Lilah appeared shaken, something that surprised her. "She's home safely but she's not fine. Not after finding out the only reason her mother wanted custody was to get her hands on her insurance money her father left her when he died."

Appearing pale, Lilah faced Macy. "I love her. I

was wrong to leave her in the first place, but the fact is that I'm broke and that money will help tremendously."

"Then who's paying for this?" Macy gestured around the beautiful hotel room with a large living room and the bedroom in the far corner.

"I haven't reached the limit on one of my credit cards."

Macy shook her head. "That's not Hannah's problem. Or mine. So let me explain the facts to you. I don't know what Dad told you about his insurance policies when you were together, but when he died, the policy money went into trust and I'm the trustee." She poked herself in the chest. "Me."

Lilah's eyes opened wide and her face grew paler, if such a thing were possible. "But I just assumed there would be monthly payments to help whoever was her guardian. And I know your grandparents left money to your father that he must have split between you and Hannah."

"Also in trust." Macy folded her arms across her chest. "You assumed wrong and you hurt your daughter in the process." She didn't wait for Lilah's reply before continuing. "Hannah's money is going to pay for her college and help her get started in life. Not to fund your lifestyle. So if you want to keep fighting me for custody, go ahead. If you win, you'll have a teenager you need to support as well as yourself."

Macy would never let Hannah suffer because of her mother's neglect, but Lilah didn't need to know that Macy would help her sister regardless of who she lived with. There was a monthly stipend, but it wasn't enough to keep Lilah in the lifestyle she wanted.

Which brought up another question. "Dad didn't have enough money to keep you happy when you were married. Why are you so eager to get your hands on it now?" Macy asked.

Lilah flushed and sat down on the sofa. Wearing a leopard-print dress and high heels, she didn't appear to be suffering from lack of money. But apparently looks were deceiving.

"You don't know how hard it is when you age. Older men with money are interested in younger women than me. And younger men assume a woman like me has a hefty income." She lifted her hands to her unlined face, courtesy of injections and fillers. "I told Rafe I was coming into a lot of money once I got custody of Hannah. She overheard him talking this morning about what we'd do when I came into money. He wanted to put her in a boarding school so she wasn't in the way."

"For God's sake, Lilah!" Macy couldn't believe that what Hannah had overheard was worse than just her mother wanting her for money. She'd also wanted to send her away.

Lilah pushed herself up from her seat, walked over to a makeshift bar, poured herself vodka, and took a sip. "That wasn't what *I* wanted. It was Rafe who said it. I've been enjoying spending time with Hannah."

Macy paced the floor in front of the woman who stood between her and her sister. "Spending time isn't the same as parenting."

"I realized that the other night while helping her clean up the party mess. I didn't envy you having to deal with the repercussions. The punishment. Hannah's anger. But then I had Rafe, who still expects me to come into money. My life is a mess!"

"And I couldn't care less."

Hand shaking, Lilah took another sip of her drink. "I don't know what to do."

Macy bit the inside of her cheek. "I'll tell you what's going to happen as far as Hannah is concerned. We both know you don't want real parental responsibility, and now you know there's no cash in it for you. Before I leave here, I want the paper you made Hannah sign stating she wants to live with you. And tomorrow you're going to call your lawyer and rescind the custody suit."

Lilah looked at her with sad, tear-filled eyes. Only Lilah knew if those tears were real. "I love her, you know," she said as she walked to a stack of papers on a table and handed Macy a sheet of paper with Hannah's familiar signature.

"You have a funny way of showing it," Macy muttered. "Don't ask me why but I'll throw you one bone. If you get your act together and want a relationship with your daughter, it's up to Hannah if she wants to have anything to do with you. I won't stand in your way if you act like an adult and a parent. But I won't let you jerk her around." As much as Macy disliked Lilah, it wasn't her place to keep Hannah from her mother.

Lilah nodded, clutching her drink in both hands.

Macy went on. "If you get in touch with Hannah again, it had better be for a real, genuine relationship. Otherwise disappear. For good this time."

She strode out without waiting for an answer. Heading down the hall to the elevator, she shook her head. She'd always known the other woman had an agenda. And to think Macy had gotten married because Lilah *assumed* Hannah came with insurance money. If only Macy had known what Lilah wanted ahead of time, then she wouldn't have married Jaxon.

Or fallen in love.

She drew in a deep breath. One half of their reason for being married was over. Her half.

Jaxon still needed the pretense of family life. And she wanted to stay married to him, but she also needed him to feel the same way about her that she did for him. She desired a real relationship and that started with honesty. Whether or not Jaxon could handle love and emotions was anyone's guess.

*   *   *

WHILE MACY WENT to deal with the wicked witch, Jaxon sat in the family room, keeping an ear out for Hannah in case she left her room and came looking for her sister. He watched an old action movie on the big screen and waited until he heard Hannah in the kitchen.

He rose and joined her.

She'd poured a bowl of cereal and milk and sat at the counter on a barstool. Though her eyes were still red, she'd cleaned up in the shower and her face was clear of black makeup.

"Mind if I join you?" he asked.

She shrugged and took another spoonful, the crunching sound loud in the silence.

Pulling the box over to him, he took a handful and popped some into his mouth. "Want to talk about it?" he asked her.

She shrugged again.

"I told you about my dad," Jaxon reminded her. "He wasn't father of the year, but I had my mother and my brothers and sister. You've got Macy."

With big eyes, Hannah met his gaze. "What if I drive her away, too? My own mother doesn't want me. Why would Macy?" She pushed the bowl away, only soggy cereal left.

Jaxon propped on an elbow and leaned close. "Has Macy gone anywhere yet? Or given you any indication that she doesn't want you? She was willing to fight your mom for you. Doesn't that prove to you how much she loves you?" he asked.

"I've been really shitty to her. I told her I'd rather live with my mom, but that was just because I was so happy Mom came back and I thought because she wanted me." She rested her chin in her hands and let out a prolonged sigh.

His heart hurt for Hannah. It was hard enough being a teenager without adding in her own mother playing head games. "It's not about you. You know that, right? Lilah's the one with the issues. You're going to be fine. You and Macy."

And him?

Was that what he wanted? To make them a real family? Could he open himself up to the feelings he knew were in his heart?

"Thanks," Hannah said, oblivious to his thoughts. "Do you love my sister?" Leave it to a teen to cut right to the point.

"It's complicated," he told her.

"Grown-ups make things complicated."

He raised his eyebrows. "Yeah? And teenagers don't?"

The smile he hadn't seen all day returned.

"True. But I see how you look at Macy." Hannah rose from her seat. "I have homework that's due tomorrow. Gotta go do it." Picking up the bowl and spoon, she walked to the sink and rinsed everything, dried it, and put it away before turning back to him. "Jaxon?"

"Yes?"

"Thanks." Impulsively, she strode over and gave him a hug before ducking her head and running out, heading for her room.

He stared after her, the teenager and her mood swings a reminder of the life he could have if he told Macy he loved her and she felt the same way.

Right now? She no longer had a reason to stay married but she would, because she'd made a bargain and he still needed the pretense of a family life. Granted, a quieter one than they'd had so far. It wasn't *real*. But it could be.

He could try and make things between them genuine. Turn their relationship into one without an expiration date looming in the future.

Head spinning, heart pounding, he picked up his phone to text Macy and see how things were going when the cell rang in his hand and Austin's name flashed on the screen.

Austin. The same brother Jaxon had sworn he'd never be like. He'd believed he wouldn't fall in love quickly like Austin had with Quinn. He'd thought he didn't need or want someone in his life who could disappoint him the way Katie had. The way his father had.

And then came Macy.

The phone rang again, startling him out of his thoughts, and he answered. "Hey! What's up?" He strode back into the family room as he spoke. "Did you keep things calm with management for me? I haven't heard from anyone, so I assume what happened last night with the party will get swept under the rug?" he asked Austin, his manager.

"It's been quiet ... which can be good or bad," Austin said, "but that's not why I'm calling."

Jaxon sat down and glanced at the television, which had the same movie from earlier playing on screen. His brother sounded serious, so he hit the mute button to avoid any distractions.

"What's going on?" Jaxon asked.

"I've had some quiet interest in you, and Eagles ownership seems willing to talk to them. I wanted to give you a heads-up."

He bolted upright in his seat. "Interest from who?"

he asked, stomach churning.

Florida was his home. His family was here. His teammates were another type of family. He'd been here for years and had hoped to play here until he retired.

"San Antonio," Austin said.

"Texas." He ran a hand through his hair. "Are you fucking kidding me?"

"They have World Series potential," Austin reminded him unnecessarily.

Nobody knew the baseball landscape as well as Jaxon.

"And that's the one thing you don't have yet." Another unnecessary reminder. Not to mention his age and time were ticking away for him to achieve that one goal. He'd all but come to terms with not earning a ring.

"I don't know how I feel about this," Jaxon muttered.

"You may not have a choice. I got a heads-up but San Antonio can be calling the Eagles as we speak. I'll work on the best package I can get for you if it comes down to it. I'm sorry, man. You may have gotten married for no reason, on your end anyway. A trade may happen anyway."

"I've got to go." Jaxon didn't want to have a conversation with Austin about marriage and Macy. He disconnected the call and tossed the phone on the sofa.

So much for thinking they could be a real family. If there was one thing he knew for sure, Macy and Hannah's life was here. Hannah went to school here. He'd seen their reactions about potentially moving school districts in state. They weren't going to pick up and go to Texas just to be with him.

And why should they?

This had been a marriage of convenience, not love. True, they'd imagined it lasting much longer than a week, but the fact was, Macy no longer needed him. Once she informed her former stepmother that Hannah didn't come with a hefty bank account she could access, Macy would secure custody of her sister. And if this trade happened, San Antonio knew what they were getting in Jaxon and wanted him anyway.

Austin was right. No marriage necessary. He could go back to his playboy ways, and Macy didn't need to be saddled with a guy who'd barely be around. Pitchers and catchers reported in a month, and he was ramping up his workouts starting this week. He was too busy to worry about a wife and a family anyway.

And even as his gut twisted at the thought of losing Macy, he knew it was for the best. Because he knew how it felt to ask the woman he loved to go with him cross country, and worse, he remembered how it felt to get turned down. And with his feelings for Macy more adult, deeper, and more real than those he'd had for Katie, he was better off being the one to walk away.

Chapter Thirteen

MACY ARRIVED BACK at Jaxon's house and heard music coming from the workout room. Leaving him alone, she headed to Hannah's room to check on her. She knocked and walked in. Hannah sat on her bed, notebook open, and she met Macy's gaze as she entered the room.

"Can we talk?" Macy asked.

Hannah nodded. "I just finished my homework."

She gathered all her books into a pile and pushed them aside, shutting her laptop, too. Without all the makeup, she looked so young and vulnerable, and Macy wanted to do her best to make this as easy as possible for her.

"I just came from seeing your mom."

Hannah looked at her with big eyes.

"And I think, in her own way, Lilah feels bad about what happened and what you overheard. It doesn't change the fact that she wanted custody of you for the wrong reasons. But I did make it clear to her that you're staying with me."

"I'm sure she didn't care once she heard there was

no money," Hannah muttered, picking at a pilled piece of her comforter.

Reaching out, Macy tucked a strand of pink hair behind her ear. "I think your mother has a lot of work to do on herself before she can think about being a parent. But I told her if she wanted a relationship, it was up to you whether or not you wanted to see her again."

Hannah blinked in surprise. "You'd let me see her?"

"I never wanted to keep you away from your mother. I just wanted you in the best place possible." She paused. "I also don't want you to be disappointed if you don't hear from her. Lilah is unpredictable." And selfish but Macy opted not to pile on the negative comments. "Are you okay?"

Hannah nodded. "What about the custody suit and the judge? And the letter?" Guilt crossed her pretty features.

"Here." Macy reached into her purse and handed Hannah the paper Lilah had returned. "This is yours."

Hannah looked at her signature and tears welled in her eyes. "I'm sorry. I was just so excited that Mom wanted me in her life again I didn't think about you."

"Honey, in many ways, your mom is like a child herself. She's impulsive, doesn't think things through, and I'm sorry to say she's manipulative. It served her purposes to give you freedom and leeway and to make me look like the strict, bad older sister so you'd want to stay with her." Drawing a deep breath, Macy told Hannah the truth. "You were used as a pawn."

And Hannah was too young and emotionally vulnerable to see it happening. "None of which means Lilah doesn't love you. It means you need to be careful about trusting her motives."

Hannah held up the paper and ripped it into pieces. "I want to stay with you."

"And you will." Macy held out her arms and Hannah slid over for a hug. "I think you've learned a lot of lessons this weekend, so we're going to start over. But no parties, no friends without asking, no sneaking out of the house. Got it?" she asked in as stern a voice as she could muster.

Hannah nodded. "Thank you."

Macy rose to her feet. "I'm going to make coffee." She started for the door when Hannah called her name. "Yes?"

"Can I go to Holly's? Her mom's out doing an errand and said she could pick me up."

Apparently Hannah had gotten over her upset with her mother. That or she wanted to talk her feelings out with a friend.

"Sure."

Hannah grabbed her phone and her fingers flew

on the keys. Her friend must have answered quickly, because within seconds, Hannah was up and out of her bed and in the process of a clothing change.

Leaving the now calm and happier teen to do her thing, Macy headed for the bedroom, where she knew Jaxon would come through to shower after he finished working out.

She settled cross-legged on the bed and was about to lean back against the pillows when her cell rang. A glance told her it was Bri.

"Hi!" she said, answering quickly. "You would not believe the day I've had so far."

"Umm, I think I would. And you're okay?" Bri sounded concerned.

Huh. Maybe she'd spoken to Jaxon and knew about Lilah and Hannah's situation. "Now that I set Lilah straight about the fact that Hannah wasn't a walking trust fund and we agreed she'd be staying with me, I'm great."

"That must be a relief," Bri agreed. "And Jaxon's probable trade? How did you take that news?" she asked.

"Trade?" Macy asked, stomach twisting at the mere mention of the word.

"Oh, shit. You don't know yet." Bri cursed up a storm on the other end of the phone.

"Know what? Was Jaxon traded and if so to

where?" Her heart rate picked up speed at the possibility.

"I shouldn't have called. I'll touch base later. Sorry!" Bri disconnected and Macy stared at the phone in her hand.

She didn't know what had happened, but whatever was going on, it wasn't good.

*   *   *

JAXON WIPED DOWN his face with a towel and climbed off the treadmill on which he'd run hard and fast. Too bad he couldn't outrun the facts of his life. Traded to San Antonio. If he wasn't married, a part of him would be excited to have a shot at a World Series win. Instead he had to tell Macy their marriage was over, something he was not looking forward to doing. Something his heart didn't want to happen. But it was for the best.

He saw Hannah leaving the house as he headed to shower. She waved on her way out.

He strode into the bedroom, surprised to see Macy had returned. She sat on the bed staring at her phone.

"Hey. How'd it go with Lilah?" he asked.

She glanced up, meeting his gaze. "Better than I expected. Money aside, I think Hannah's impromptu party last night showed Lilah she wasn't ready to handle a teenager. I got Hannah's letter back, and

Lilah will cancel her petition for custody." A wide, satisfied smile took hold and he was thrilled for her.

Genuinely as happy as if the news were his own.

"That's amazing. Seriously. I'm so happy for you."

She rose to her feet. "You don't sound happy."

"Reading my mood?" he asked, catching the light snark in his voice and wincing. It wasn't her fault his life was changing at lightning speed and he had to figure out a way to tell her.

She bit down on her lower lip. "Bri mentioned something about a trade."

He'd wrapped the towel around his neck and pulled on the ends. Leave it to his sister to beat him to giving Macy the news.

"Austin called this morning right after you left. San Antonio is interested in me and the Eagles are considering it."

"San Antonio, *Texas*?" Macy asked, her voice rising, the panic in her voice confirming his thoughts. She'd want no part of moving.

"That's the one." He walked past her and into the bathroom, planning to close the door and take a shower, but she followed him in.

"Don't walk out on me. We have to discuss this."

"Actually, we really don't. You married me in order to get custody of Hannah, and that's taken care of. I married you to help me show the management of the

Eagles I'd change, settle down, and quit going viral with my *antics*," he said with air quotes around the last word. "If this trade happens, San Antonio knows who I am and would be taking me regardless." He tossed the neck towel onto the counter.

"Oh, I see. It's that simple? You go your way, I'll go mine? Marriage over? Just like that?" She snapped her fingers.

He couldn't help but grin at her sass. He found it hot and sexy.

"Quit smirking. This isn't funny."

"No, it's not. But you have to admit we both got what we needed from the marriage. We just thought the arrangement would last longer. Now you can have your freedom back."

She glared at him, taking him off guard. "You mean you can have yours. You're the playboy. You're the one who's missing your old life."

"Whoa. I never said that." In fact, not once since agreeing to marry Macy had he wished for his single life. She filled him in ways he hadn't known he needed.

"Well, you're not giving me a choice in what happens next, either. You're telling me we're through, so of course I think you're eager to pick up a different woman every night."

Fury sounded in her voice that made him step back and wonder if he hadn't misjudged her. And if he

231

had the guts to find out. Her words had stayed with him. *All I'm saying is don't let the rest of your life be defined by something that happened when you were young.*

He was such an ass. He was a Major League pitcher and he was afraid of going after what he wanted? "What if I asked you to go with me to Texas? You and Hannah?" he asked and held his breath.

Her mouth opened wide. "Yes, Jaxon, of course we'll go with you. I love you, you big idiot! I don't want you to go to Texas without me."

He studied her in shock. "What about your life?"

Her brown gaze met his. "What life? My work is mobile. In a short week, my life has become about you and my sister. And she might not be happy initially but she'll adjust. She'll just make our lives hell until that happens."

He grinned, unable to believe this had all been so simple. All the angst and drama and here they were. "Go back to what you said before."

"Which thing?"

"You love me?" he asked, wanting to hear her say the words again.

She grasped his face and cupped his cheeks in her hand. "I love you, Jaxon Prescott. Now are you going to say it back or do I have to drag the words out of you?"

He lifted her by the waist and sat her on the counter, legs dangling, and he stepped between them. "I love you, Macy Prescott."

"And you'll trust in us from here on out? Because I need you in my life. Both Hannah and I need you."

"I need you, too. And you showed me how to trust. We're a team, for good or bad," he assured her, and then his lips were on hers.

He devoured her, making sure to leave no doubt in her mind that not only did he love her but he wanted her in his life forever.

Sliding his hands beneath her dress, he hooked his fingers into her panties and eased them down her legs, then pulled her to the edge of the counter. Her slick pussy was wet and ready for him. It took him mere seconds to remove his workout shorts and boxers, his cock hard, thick, and ready to enter her.

She arched her hips, giving him easy access, then, gazes locked, he slammed into her. She gasped and squeezed him tight in her heat.

"Oh, God."

"Like that?" He slid out and thrust back in, holding on to her hips so her head didn't bang against the mirror behind her. She gripped his shoulders and locked her legs behind his back, urging him on.

And this time when their eyes met, he didn't back away from the feelings inside him or letting her see the emotions she brought forth. And when she came, the squeeze of her around him took him up and over the edge along with her.

They were cleaning up when he heard Hannah's voice. "I forgot my phone!" she yelled out.

Macy yelped and jumped off the counter as Jaxon slammed the bathroom door shut behind them.

"Oh, my God. That was close." Macy closed her eyes and groaned.

"Macy?" Hannah called from what sounded like inside the master bedroom.

"Be right out!" She glanced at Jaxon, her cheeks burning bright with embarrassment. "Last opportunity to change your mind," she said with a grin.

"Not a chance. We're a family. And you, Macy, are mine."

*   *   *

TWO WEEKS LATER, Macy, with Jaxon's permission and pushing, made some changes to add more warmth and personality to the family room and other places around the interior of the home.

Hannah had surprised them with printed photos from the night of the gala, and those pictures along with the wedding photos held prominent places on shelves and counters. They were a true family, and despite how quickly it had happened, she couldn't deny it was all real.

Including the moody teenager. At first, on being given the news that they might move to Texas, she'd slammed her door, cried, called her friends, and had a tantrum. All expected and Macy spent a week convincing her they'd love it there and she would make new friends. To everyone's surprise, the Eagles changed their mind at the last possible second, deciding they wanted to keep their star pitcher through the end of his career.

All the fan pages online and the radio talk shows had slammed management for trading their franchise player, and in the end, they'd agreed and canceled the trade. Macy knew how much Jaxon would have liked a World Series ring, but she knew he wanted to retire as a Miami Eagle even more. Loyalty was everything to the Prescott men.

Her man, especially.

How did Hannah take the news? Macy and Jaxon had assumed she'd be thrilled, but true to teenage unpredictability, she'd had a fit that she'd just accepted the idea of moving and now they were staying put. An hour later, Ruby came over with Holly, and the girls were celebrating at the pool.

Teenagers.

Since Jaxon had ramped up his workouts in preparation for pitchers and catchers reporting for practice for the season, Macy kept busy with work and adding to her life with both relatives and friends. She and Lizzie spent a day together, and Macy decided to put her father's house up for sale and put half the money away for Hannah, half in her own savings. And Jaxon's mother and Bri had taken her for lunch to officially welcome her to the family. Considering she and Hannah had no family of their own, everyone's efforts meant the world to Macy.

As for Lilah, she'd disappeared again, but Macy knew she'd be back one day. The nature of the beast. She'd explained to Hannah the concept of accepting someone for who and what they were, and they'd deal with her mother if and when she surfaced again.

Life was so much brighter than it had been a mere month or so ago, and for that she was grateful. She stepped back from the frames she'd put in the kitchen because the counterspace was so expansive and smiled with appreciation.

Just then, she heard the sound of the garage door leading to the house and saw Jaxon walk in, hair almost dry because he'd showered at the stadium, a pair of black track pants low on his hips, and a tee shirt that lifted thanks to his duffel hefted over one shoulder, revealing a strip of hair along his happy trail.

Her belly churned with excitement at the sight of him as it always did, more so since they'd admitted their feelings. He strode up beside her, wrapped an arm around her waist, pulling her into him for a long, deep kiss.

"Miss me?" he asked when they came up for air.

"Always." She smiled. "So? How does it look?"

He took in the edge of the counter with a new cookie jar and the *family* photographs and grinned. "Love them. Just like I love you."

Her heart skipped a beat. She'd never get tired of hearing him say the words. "I love you, too."

He replied with a more thorough kiss, his tongue sliding past her lips, allowing her to drink in his taste, and she rubbed her body against his.

"Gross! God. Can't you keep it in the bedroom?" Hannah stormed in and headed straight for the refrigerator for a snack.

"Hi, Hannah."

She peeked her head out of the fridge. "Hello, Jaxon." She pulled out a can of soda. "I'm going back to my room so you two go back to whatever you were doing." She waved a hand dismissively.

Jaxon met Macy's gaze and grinned. "This is called living the good life."

"Says the man who said he wouldn't get married or make a commitment in this lifetime."

He shook his head and laughed. "This is the one and only time I'll admit to being wrong."

"Arrogant man."

"Good thing I have you to keep me in line," he said and kissed her once more, reminding her that all good things in life were worth waiting for.

Epilogue

J AXON JOINED HIS siblings at Allstars. It was the first
time they'd hung out together since Braden's return,
and he was thrilled to have the family together. Bri had
given them the brush-off, telling the boys to go hang
out. He knew Braden and Bri would have their own
catch-up time.

Braden cracked his knuckles, a definite indication
that his brother was stressed. He'd been doing it since
he was a kid. Considering he'd just returned and was
probably floundering with what to do next, Jaxon
didn't blame him for being uptight. Braden had rented
a house with his friend Hudson Northfield, whose
decision to join Doctors without Borders had prompt-
ed Braden, who'd always had a soft spot for those in
need, to do the same.

Shifting in his seat, Braden glanced around, obviously trying to get comfortable. After the tents he'd
slept in, no doubt everywhere he went took getting
used to. Jaxon was just glad his brother was home and
hoped it was for good.

"So what are you two thinking of doing career-wise?" Austin asked before taking a sip of his club soda.

"Hudson and I have a meeting tomorrow with a health clinic in downtown Miami where we want to volunteer," Braden said.

Hudson raised a glass in acknowledgment.

"What about taking the opportunity from Ian as head doctor for the Thunder?" Jaxon asked about their cousin's football team.

Ian had offered Braden the position of head team physician, taking over for Dr. Jonas, who was currently in prison after pleading guilty to numerous crimes, not the least of which was injecting Damon with performance-enhancing drugs without his knowledge in order to obtain money to pay off gambling debts and money owed to the IRS. He'd also generously offered Hudson a position as well.

Braden stiffened. Obviously this wasn't a subject he wanted to discuss. "I'm considering it. He needs an answer soon."

"Hudson?" he asked his brother's friend.

The other man rolled his shoulders. "Same. It's a big change from the work I was previously doing. I need to know it will work for me before I make a commitment."

Jaxon respected that, just as he understood why this was a difficult decision for his brother. Braden had never chosen anything to do with sports, thanks to the way his father had treated him. Jesse had had no respect for Braden's intelligence, caring only that he couldn't nor did he want to be a football player. Jaxon got why Braden might want to spite Jesse Prescott, but Braden needed a job now that he was home and this was a good one. Not to mention, Jesse was long gone, even if the scars he'd left were never forgotten.

"What's holding you back?" Austin asked.

"A few things," Braden said vaguely.

"Including the fact that Willow works there as an athletic trainer?" Damon chimed in with the question and Jaxon winced.

Even he knew better than to bring up Braden's ex. All Jaxon knew was they'd been together and then one day Braden announced he was leaving for two years, taking everyone from his family to his girlfriend by surprise. From what he'd seen of her, he thought she'd been a nice woman and a good compliment to Braden.

Hudson remained silent. Considering he'd been with Braden after the breakup, he probably knew more than Jaxon did about the fallout.

"You do realize she'd have to ultimately answer to you," Damon added.

Braden shrugged. "I mean, it won't be easy working with her considering things didn't end on a good note, but it won't affect whether or not I take the position. Besides, she's a professional. She'll deal just like I will." If the long sip of his scotch was any indication, he didn't believe the words he spoke as much as he wanted to.

Jaxon couldn't help but notice his sibling was being deliberately vague with the emotional aspect of his answers, whether because he was confused about his next steps or he wanted to keep the information to himself, Jaxon didn't know.

"Maybe her presence will sway you toward taking the job?" Damon asked.

Jaxon had to admit, his sibling didn't give up.

Glancing at Braden, Jaxon wondered the same thing. Was he sorry he'd left her? Or relieved? Braden kept his feelings close. Always had.

"When is your wedding?" Braden clearly changed the topic and looked to Austin for an answer.

Austin grinned, obviously happy with the chance to talk about his future with Quinn. "Valentine's Day at the Meridian Hotel. Between our family and Quinn's, we have a boatload of people. We needed more room than our house could provide."

Braden sat up straighter in his seat. "You're getting married at Robert Dare's hotel?" Out of the loop, Braden sounded shocked.

Robert Dare was Paul's brother, Ian's estranged father, and the man who had had two families at the same time, in secret.

Austin chuckled. "I forgot you wouldn't have heard. Robert had to sell his hotels to help pay for the divorce settlement. Savannah, his second wife, took him for a bundle. Apparently they had a prenup. She learned from being his mistress first. Shockingly, he signed it, thinking he'd be faithful. Stupid given the old adage *once a cheater, always a cheater.*" He shook his head. "Could have saved himself a fortune."

Braden laughed. "The man always was an ass."

Jaxon couldn't argue the point. "I guess you don't know who purchased the hotels, either. The Dirty Dares."

"I still can't believe you call them that," Austin muttered.

Jaxon ignored him. "They all went in on the hotel venture together. But with Harrison busy acting and Asher having his hands full with Dirty Dare Vodka, Nick, Zach, and Emery are deciding who wants to work the business full-time."

"Sounds like I've missed a lot."

Jaxon swung an arm around him. "The good news is you'll have plenty of time to catch up. You're not sure about the job with Ian, but you're not leaving, are you?"

Braden immediately shook his head.

Good, Jaxon thought. His brother was home to

stay.

"Glad to hear it," Austin said, rising from his seat. "I'm going to get home to Quinn and the baby."

"On that note, I'm out of here, too." Damon stood. "I told Evie I wouldn't be home late."

"I'm beat." Hudson, who hadn't spoken much during the evening, also rose to his feet. "I'm sure I'll be seeing more of you all."

And Jaxon hoped to learn more about the enigmatic man his brother had followed to foreign countries.

Braden looked to Jaxon, the only brother who hadn't announced his departure. Sensing his sibling needed an ear, he shook his head. "I'll stick around awhile if you will."

"I'm here."

Jaxon waited until everyone left before turning to his brother. "You've been quiet. And not very forthcoming about what's going on in your head. If you need a shoulder, I'm here."

With a sigh, Braden rested his back against the chair.

"Is it about Jesse?" He'd stopped thinking of him as Dad and it hadn't been difficult.

Braden shook his head. "His words are always with me, but I won't let him decide what I do with my life. But me ending up in sports? It's just ironic and I need to come to terms with the idea, you know?"

Jaxon nodded. "But volunteering downtown will fill the need you have to help people. It can be the best of both worlds."

"It isn't traveling and I've gotten used to that. I like going to different countries and coming to the aid of people in need."

Jaxon spent so much time on the road he valued his home time more than ever. He hoped Braden would come to appreciate the value of staying in one place near the people he loved, too.

"No one says you have to take this position with the Thunder forever. If it doesn't work for you, so be it."

Linking his fingers behind his head, Braden met his gaze. "You make the decision sound easy."

"That's because it is. Unless there's another reason you're hesitating." Jaxon paused. "Like Willow?"

Braden groaned, running a hand through his hair. "To be honest? Yeah. The thing is, we were exclusive but not serious. I wasn't ready for something intense. Which doesn't excuse my sudden decision to leave the country for two years. It came out of nowhere and I get why she was upset."

Jaxon mulled over his brother's words. "You two keep in touch?"

With a shake of his head, Braden said, "She didn't

answer my calls or texts. And to be honest, I didn't realize how much I cared about her until I was away. By then she was ignoring me and I gave up. It wasn't like I could do much from a foreign country."

"And now?"

"Who knows." He finished the last of his drink. "But if I take the job, I guess I'll find out. Anyway, I'm done talking about myself. It's time to get out of here. You ready?"

Jaxon nodded. "I'm going home to my wife." And he hoped one day Braden could get his head on straight, figure out what he wanted out of life, and maybe say the same.

Thanks for reading! Continue this series with Dare to Stay!

Keep reading for a sneak peek!

DARE TO STAY EXCERPT

B RADEN PRESCOTT'S SUIT felt stiff and scratchy, a far cry from the loose scrubs he'd worn for the last two years with Doctors Without Borders. He pulled at the knot on his tie as he waited for the press conference to begin, announcing him as head team general doctor for the Miami Thunder. Beside him was his cousin and team owner, Ian Dare.

"Nervous?" Ian asked, an understanding look on his face.

"More like uncomfortable." And stressed but Braden wasn't about to admit as much. Instead he rolled his shoulders in a futile effort to unwind and believe this new phase would work out.

"Excuse me. I need to talk to someone before the press conference starts." Ian placed a hand on Braden's shoulder before walking away, leaving him to ponder his sudden life change.

It was ironic that he'd accepted this position considering sports medicine had never been on his list of career choices. And for good reason. He'd steered clear of anything that reminded him of the father who'd raised him, because Jesse Prescott had belittled him for his brain, wanting only sons capable of smashing into other men on a football field.

Four of his siblings had ended up in sports in one way or another, and Braden was proud of all they'd accomplished, but it had never been his calling. However, now that he was back in town, he needed a job as much as Ian needed a general practitioner physician he could trust. The last man who'd held the job had betrayed his oath and the people he was supposed to care for.

From the wings, Braden glanced out into the audience of reporters in the front seats and team members filing into the chairs in the back. He caught sight of Hudson Northfield, his best friend, whose idea it had been to join Doctors Without Borders. He'd returned to the States with Braden and come to Florida instead of heading home to New York, where his high-pressured family resided. At Braden's recommendation, Ian had hired Hudson as a team physician, meaning he'd be staying in Florida and not moving home.

But Braden wasn't looking for Hudson when he scanned the crowd. He was searching for a certain blonde-haired, blue-eyed siren he'd left behind. He and Willow James, now head of the Athletic Training Department for the Thunder, had been a couple before Hudson had approached him about joining Doctors Without Border, or MSF as it was known, Médicins Sans Frontières.

He'd been the odd man out at home, the only Prescott brother who hadn't been into sports, and the opportunity to travel and help people in need, while carving out his own niche in life, had been too much of a lure to turn down. At the time, he'd thought Willow, with whom he'd been in an exclusive but not overly serious relationship, would accept the notion that he'd be gone for two years. That they'd see one another when possible. He'd been wrong.

She'd listened, nodded, told him to have a nice life, and walked out, stunning him with how easily she'd dismissed him. Although looking back and knowing her foster care background, he should have dug deeper into her reaction. Instead he'd left despite knowing he'd hurt her with his sudden pronouncement, not taking into consideration the fact that she probably felt abandoned and had thrown up her walls. And though he didn't regret the time he'd spent abroad, he knew he'd done irreparable damage to their relationship.

When Ian had offered him the job, he'd done his research on who he'd be working with, already knowing she'd been with the Thunder when he left. And maybe he'd scanned her social media. A little. The glimpses being the equivalent of a punch in the gut as he realized how much he'd given up when he'd left.

He hadn't realized the depth of his feelings for her until he'd been gone. Hadn't thought he'd miss her as much as he had. And considering her silence in response to his early texts and the calls she'd let go unanswered, she hadn't forgiven him for his last-minute decision to leave.

As the head of the Thunder's Athletic Training Department, she'd be answering to him as lead team physician, something he doubted would make her happy. But they were both adults and professionals. They'd make things work.

And if he had his way, he'd win back her trust.

Somehow.

* * *

WILLOW JAMES WALKED down the hall of the Miami Thunder Football Stadium, headed to the area reserved for press conferences. Ian Dare would be announcing the new head physician. Normally the information would be revealed via press release to the public and in a private team meeting, but given the fact that the former doctor, Peter Jonas, was currently doing time in prison for defrauding the IRS, taking a bribe to pay gambling debts, and injecting the Thunder's star quarterback with banned substances in return for money to pay off his loans, the team needed to make a statement.

As she turned a corner toward the press room, she passed life-size photographs of the Thunder's star players, a tribute that followed them from the old stadium. Because this one was new, the smell of paint still permeated the air around her.

She'd been around the organization for a while, had done two summers and a full-year internship with the team prior to working as one of the trainers for years before being promoted to lead last month. She knew how fortunate she was to have found a place for herself with the Thunder. There were many trainers like her with a stellar academic record, but it had been her relationship with Dr. Peter Jonas, her one-time foster father, that had given her an in. Having known him for years, she'd never suspected he was capable of such betrayal.

His wife, Bella, was destroyed, and since the Jonases were the last of five foster homes Willow had been in, and by then she'd been near to adulthood, she had an ongoing relationship with them, unlike the other families who'd taken her in and easily let her go. She kept in close touch with Bella and spoke to her often. If there was anyone in her life Willow trusted, it was

Bella Jonas, and she'd look out for her any way she had to.

Peter was another person who'd let her down. Life taught her that it was in her best interest to keep people at a distance, and every time she broke that rule, she'd been hurt in the end.

Given Damon Prescott's status, the news about Doc had spread fast, hitting the team hard. Ian had withheld the name of the new doctor until announcement time, and she'd find out along with everyone else in a few minutes.

She stepped into the room, the crowd of reporters buzzing with anticipation over the upcoming news. Scanning the seats in the back, she walked toward the closest person to her in the Athletic Training Department, Steffy Hughes, a petite brunette who was a few years younger than Willow's thirty-one. But they'd been friends for almost two years, shared drinks after work, attended exercise classes together, and bonded over their love of sports. As the only two women in the training department, they'd gravitated toward each other, and Willow had let Steffy in more than she did most people.

"Glad I'm not late. I was doing paperwork and lost track of time," Willow said as she slid in beside her friend.

Steffy shook her head. "Not at all. Any ideas who

they're bringing on?"

"Not a clue. I haven't heard of any shake-ups at other teams, so they're not grabbing anyone we'd know of that way. I just know that Mr. Dare wants to make a statement that we're starting fresh and with someone who has no possibility of being corrupted in any way. He hated the scandal that hit us."

"Didn't we all," Steffy said. "Everyone has been tiptoeing around here. I'm ready for a change in atmosphere. I know Doc's second in charge has been holding down the fort, but everyone knows he's looking to move west with his family. We're mid-season and need a qualified doctor in charge."

"Amen," Willow said, just as Ian Dare strode into the room and stood at the podium.

An imposing man in a black suit with a white shirt, top button opened, Ian was also extremely good-looking. He exuded power by virtue of his attitude and backed up his controlling demeanor with a solid work ethic, so everyone respected him. With his dark brown hair and very familiar indigo eyes, every time she saw Ian, she was reminded of the man she wanted to forget.

The man she'd dubbed *he who shall not be named.* The well-known words fit the guy who'd easily dumped her and taken off for parts unknown. Ironically, *he* was also related to Ian, information that had come to light after he'd left for a stint with Doctors Without Borders. A decision he'd made seemingly out of nowhere.

Not that they'd been looking toward the future, but she'd had strong feelings for him that had been growing by the day. She'd let herself start to fall for him despite knowing better, and she'd thought she knew what his plans were and had foolishly let herself believe they'd included her. Just another time in her life she'd been let down and left behind. Something she would not let happen again.

"Welcome and thank you for joining me here today along with Coach Carson." Ian gestured to the man beside him who ran the team before going into a long speech about the integrity of the Miami Thunder organization and everyone who worked for and was associated with them.

She'd zoned out for a few minutes when clapping around her alerted her to the fact that she'd missed something important.

Shaking her head, she looked up and watched in shock as *he* strode onto the stage. Dr. Braden Prescott. The man who'd walked out on her two years ago and apparently the new head physician for the Miami Thunder.

Her heart pounded so hard in her chest she heard the sound in her ears. He looked scrumptious in his dark suit and the short scruff of beard he hadn't had last time she saw him. As if no time had passed, her traitorous body responded to his presence.

"Oh my God, he's hot," Steffy said, waving her hand in front of her face at the same time Willow spoke. "Oh, shit, that's my ex."

"What?" Steffy asked too loudly, then lowered her voice. "You were with that gorgeous guy?" Steffy had been hired not long after Braden left, and Willow had already locked up her feelings and closed them in a box in her mind, never to be opened again.

Willow nodded. "We were together for a year, but I haven't seen him in two."

"Well, you'll be working with him now. Oh no! What will Cole think?" Steffy asked of the doctor on staff Willow was currently dating.

Her stomach twisted at the thought. She and Cole Walsh had just started going out. She was keeping things casual, and he respected her need to go slow. She hadn't slept with anyone since Braden because she hadn't met any man who made her want to allow him that close. She thought Cole had potential. Now she had Braden to contend with, although given how easily he'd taken off, she doubted he'd be interested in her now. And she wasn't into second chances after being left.

"Your life suddenly got complicated," Steffy mut-

255

tered.

No shit, she thought.

"Can you handle it?" her friend asked.

"Doesn't look like I have a choice." Willow glanced at the podium once more and realized Braden was staring directly at her.

As he stood next to his cousin, the family resemblance was clear. Dark hair, strong jaw, full lips… She even remembered how good he smelled, the scent of his woodsy cologne, and the feel of his body against hers. She closed her eyes and wondered how in the fresh hell this had happened. The man she'd spent two years trying to forget would now be permanently in her orbit?

She grabbed her phone and whispered, "I'm going to get ready for my next patient." It was a lie. She didn't have anyone on schedule, and Steffy probably knew it.

But she needed to get out of this room full of people and hole up in her office, where she could catch her breath and shore up her defenses against Braden Prescott, MD.

* * *

BRADEN WATCHED WILLOW stand up and walk out the side door of the press room, and his sole goal was to get through this conference and find her. He'd noted the shock in her expression upon seeing him and kicked himself for not warning her ahead of time. Not that she'd have taken his call, but he could have texted or left a message.

She looked beautiful, her blonde hair tied in a ponytail, her face lightly made up. He couldn't see what she wore besides the black long-sleeve workout top that clung to her curves. If he had any doubt about his feelings, if he'd wondered whether time was making him long for someone and seeing her would shake him out of his stupor, he now knew.

He wanted her back.

Forcing himself to focus, he answered questions about his background. Discussed how he'd finished college early, fast-tracked med school and his residency, worked at a clinic downtown, then done his stint with MSF. He was also board-certified in sports medicine, something he'd done because of his brothers' career choices. He wanted to be available if needed. Now he was home and ready for the opportunity to head the team.

Had family strings been pulled in his hiring? Ian had answered that question. Probably but Ian was adamant that Braden was trustworthy and that mattered when his team had been shattered by Dr. Jonas's betrayal. He'd ended questions there.

Braden strode off the stage, determined to see Willow, only to be waylaid by team members wanting to welcome him, and he had to take time for the introductions and conversations with the people he'd be working with in the upcoming days and weeks. They needed to get to know and trust him with their bodies and injuries, and he wouldn't shirk those responsibilities in favor of his love life.

"Good job!" a familiar voice said with warmth and excitement.

"Brianne!" He turned to face his twin with a grin, extremely happy to see her.

Being away from his family had been difficult. Being separated from his twin sister had been twice as hard. He and Bri had a bond no one but them could really understand. Since he'd been home, she'd been busy with clients and planning their brother Jaxon's wedding, while he'd been organizing his new life, renting an apartment, and conducting meetings with Ian about this job.

"I couldn't miss my brother's big introduction." She pulled him into a tight hug. "I'm so glad you're back, and I know you're going to kick ass at this position."

She stepped back and tucked her dark hair behind one ear. "Okay, why do you look stressed? Is this too much for you?" She gestured around the room still full of people.

He shook his head. "I'm fine. There's just someone I need to see, and I haven't had a second to slip out of here."

"Aah. Willow?"

He inclined his head. "Willow."

Bri had known Willow from the year that she and Braden had been involved. She was a publicist at their brother Austin's firm, Dare Nation, and many of her clients were Thunder players, so she kept up with staffing and roster changes. She'd know that Willow was now head of the Athletic Training Department. The two women had gotten along well, but Willow tended to keep people at a distance, and Bri had respected her boundaries. Braden had just begun to break through her outer shell to the soft woman beneath when the MSF opportunity had come up.

"You're distracted. Come. I'll walk with you to the training area, then I'll go bother some of my clients about their lack of social media presence."

He chuckled. "I wouldn't want to be them."

Bri was the best at what she did, because before she took on a client, she laid out exactly what she both needed and expected of them. Once they agreed, she rode them hard to get the optimal result, but that could make her a pain in the ass, which was what they paid her to be.

She nudged Braden in the ribs. "They love me."

He rolled his eyes just as Hudson walked up and joined them. "Good job," he said, slapping Braden on the back.

"I was just telling him that," Bri said.

Hudson smiled at Bri. "You look beautiful today. The royal blue in your shirt brings out your eyes."

"Is that your way of flirting?" Bri asked, sounding almost coy.

Braden narrowed his gaze. "I think it was a compliment. I'm not so sure he'd make a play in front of your brother. Your *twin*."

That earned him another nudge in his ribs. "I don't need you protecting me like I'm five years old."

Hudson laughed. "You two bicker like siblings. I'm complimenting a beautiful woman. Although if I wanted to date her, I'd think you'd approve of your best friend asking your sister out?" Hudson threw the volley back and smiled at them both. "See you later," he said, and before Braden could reply, he strode off, shaking his head.

"You made me look like I can't handle myself. Like a child. Don't do that," Bri said, obviously annoyed with him.

He held up both hands. "I'm sorry. Hudson's a good guy. It was just instinct to protect you."

"Well, as I tell my four brothers, I don't need protection!"

"I'll always look out for you," Braden said, being deliberately stubborn because it was true.

She let out an exasperated noise. "How about we go find Willow and put your love life front and center?" she asked, clearly still worked up over his interference.

"Sounds like a plan," he muttered.

They headed out of the room, and although Ian had given him a tour of the stadium during off hours, he was glad to have Bri by his side directing him. Even if she was still annoyed with him.

After passing through the Hall of Fame, which included Austin, who had retired as a wide receiver, he thought maybe one day Damon, the current quarterback, would also hang on these hallowed walls.

Bri stopped at a point where they could go straight or right. "Since I doubt you want to face her for the first time with your sister holding your hand, I'll leave you here. Down that hall and the room on the right. Her name's on the door."

"Come on, Bri. Don't be mad at me." He used his most cajoling voice.

She frowned but he could tell it was forced. "I'm not mad. You're just annoying."

"But you love me." He kissed her cheek. "Talk to you soon."

He turned and headed down the hall, scanning the

doors with name plaques on each. He realized from his previous tour that Willow's office probably connected on another side to the gym area where the trainers worked with the athletes.

Drawing a deep breath, he knocked on her door.

*   *   *

WILLOW RETURNED TO her office and tried to immerse herself in the information on her computer about current players and their injuries but kept spacing out. She found it hard to focus when all she could see was Braden standing on the stage, looking so good in his suit and new scruff of beard. She hated how her body still responded to a mere look at him.

She clicked on the mouse of her computer when a knock sounded on her door, no doubt Steffy coming by to gossip about her blurting out her past relationship with the team's new doctor.

"Come in!" she called out. She closed out the page she was looking at and glanced up as her door opened and Braden walked inside, shutting the door behind him. Her stomach flipped at the sight of him, and she rose to her feet.

"Willow, it's really good to see you." He stepped toward her, his arms out, clearly intending to hug her. Being in his embrace and inhaling his sexy scent was the last thing she could handle, and she held out a hand to stop him from coming any closer.

He stopped, respecting her boundaries, and she let out a sigh of relief. "How are you, Braden?"

"I'm good. Settling in. How have you been?" he asked, those violet eyes staring into hers.

"Also good. Enjoying my promotion, which reminds me. Congratulations on your new position." She folded her arms across her chest in an effort to keep a barrier between them.

"Thank you. I'm looking forward to getting to know everyone and traveling with the team."

God, she hadn't let herself think about the fact that they'd be on away trips together, as well.

"You look great," he said, his gaze taking her in, and though she wore a pair of black leggings and a Thunder fitted shirt, she felt naked beneath his stare.

"Thanks." She didn't want things to get personal nor did she desire a conversation about when he had returned or how his time with MSF had been. "So what can I do for you?"

"First, I wanted to say hello. Second, we'll be working together, and I thought we should clear the air."

She inclined her head. "Don't worry. My entire staff will keep you up-to-date on every player." She turned away from him and stepped toward her desk, away from the scent of his cologne that would now linger in her personal space.

He groaned and ran a hand through his hair, messing it in ways she'd seen when they'd finished a round in bed. Clearing her throat, she sat down in her chair, hoping he'd take it as a dismissal.

"Willow, look. I'm sorry about how things ended between us and I'd like to talk." He strode closer to her desk.

"There's nothing to discuss unless it's about the team." She answered before he could settle himself on the corner as he'd clearly been about to do. "We're colleagues and I'll be professional. I'll talk to you when I need to, and nothing will fall through the cracks, but I want to be clear. There is nothing personal between us. Not anymore." Resting her hands on her lap, she curled them into fists, her nails digging into her skin.

This conversation was costing her. Her pulse was racing and her stomach churning. She resented the fact that this man could still have a hold over her in any way.

"That's where you're wrong." He grasped the arm of her chair and spun her to face him, then braced his hands behind her shoulders.

His face was close to hers, his lips so near if she moved at all she'd be kissing him.

"I can see the emotion you're holding back," he said in a deep voice. "We have unresolved issues, and you can be sure we'll be discussing them. In the meantime, how about a tour of the place?"

She narrowed her gaze. "Didn't Ian walk you through the stadium when he was trying to sway you to take this job?"

"I have a bad sense of direction. I need another one." He stood up straight, and she could breathe now that they weren't face-to-face. He was still too close for comfort, she thought, as she rolled her eyes at his blatant lie. They both knew he had an excellent sense of direction.

"I would also like you to run me through the daily schedule and fill me in on anything I need to know from your perspective so I can hit the ground running. I know the team is home this weekend, but we have an away game the weekend after. Anything you can clarify for me will be great."

"Fine." She couldn't say no to his request, so she cleared her throat and waited for him to get the message and step out of her personal space.

Once he did, she held back the sigh of relief and pushed herself to her feet. "I'll show you around, and then we can go over the players who are possibly on the IRL. Injured Reserve List, in case you don't know."

"I did grow up in a sports-centered house. I'm aware of the terms. Just let me leave my jacket here. I can't stand how stuffy I feel." He shrugged off the jacket and, to her surprise, tugged at his tie next.

"What are you doing?"

"Relaxing now that the press conference is over." He pulled at his tie, loosening it, then undoing it completely, and to her frustration, undid two buttons on his shirt, revealing the sprinkling of dark chest hair she used to lay her hand on after always amazing sex.

Shit, shit, shit. She had to stop thinking of the past.

He laid the jacket over the arm of her chair and added his tie on top.

"Ready?" she asked, trying not to show how much he affected her.

"Sure am." He grinned as if he could absolutely read her mind and winked.

She shivered and hoped he didn't notice her hardening nipples. The damned man. "Then let's go."

He gestured to the door. "Ladies first."

He always had been a gentleman. She stepped ahead of him, feeling the burn of his stare on her back as she walked out of the room.

Want even more Carly books?

CARLY'S BOOKLIST by Series – visit:
https://www.carlyphillips.com/CPBooklist

Sign up for Carly's Newsletter:
https://www.carlyphillips.com/CPNewsletter

Join Carly's Corner on Facebook:
https://www.carlyphillips.com/CarlysCorner

Carly on Facebook:
https://www.carlyphillips.com/CPFanpage

Carly on Instagram:
https://www.carlyphillips.com/CPInstagram

Carly's Booklist

The Dare Series

Dare to Love Series
Book 1: Dare to Love (Ian & Riley)
Book 2: Dare to Desire (Alex & Madison)
Book 3: Dare to Touch (Dylan & Olivia)
Book 4: Dare to Hold (Scott & Meg)
Book 5: Dare to Rock (Avery & Grey)
Book 6: Dare to Take (Tyler & Ella)
A Very Dare Christmas – Short Story (Ian & Riley)

** Sienna Dare gets together with Ethan Knight in **The Knight Brothers** (Dare Me Tonight).*

** Jason Dare gets together with Faith in the **Sexy Series** (More Than Sexy).*

Dare NY Series (NY Dare Cousins)
Book 1: Dare to Surrender (Gabe & Isabelle)
Book 2: Dare to Submit (Decklan & Amanda)
Book 3: Dare to Seduce (Max & Lucy)

The Knight Brothers
Book 1: Take Me Again (Sebastian & Ashley)
Book 2: Take Me Down (Parker & Emily)
Book 3: Dare Me Tonight (Ethan Knight & Sienna Dare)
Novella: Take The Bride (Sierra & Ryder)
Take Me Now – Short Story (Harper & Matt)

The Sexy Series
Book 1: More Than Sexy (Jason Dare & Faith)

Book 2: Twice As Sexy (Tanner & Scarlett)
Book 3: Better Than Sexy (Landon & Vivienne)
Novella: Sexy Love (Shane & Amber)

Dare Nation
Book 1: Dare to Resist (Austin & Quinn)
Book 2: Dare to Tempt (Damon & Evie)
Book 3: Dare to Play (Jaxon & Macy)
Book 4: Dare to Stay (Brandon & Willow)
Novella: Dare to Tease (Hudson & Brianne)

Paul Dare's sperm donor kids

Kingston Family
Book 1: Just One Night (Linc Kingston & Jordan Greene)
Book 2: Just One Scandal (Chloe Kingston & Beck Daniels)
Book 3: Just One Chance (Xander Kingston & Sasha Keaton)
Book 4: Just One Spark (Dash Kingston & Cassidy Forrester)
Book 5: Just One Wish (Axel Forrester)
Book 6: Just One Dare (Aurora Kingston & Nick Dare)
Book 7: Just One Kiss
Book 8: Just One Taste

For the most recent Carly books, visit CARLY'S BOOKLIST page
www.carlyphillips.com/CPBooklist

Other Indie Series

Billionaire Bad Boys
Book 1: Going Down Easy
Book 2: Going Down Hard
Book 3: Going Down Fast
Book 4: Going In Deep
Going Down Again – Short Story

Hot Heroes Series
Book 1: Touch You Now
Book 2: Hold You Now
Book 3: Need You Now
Book 4: Want You Now

Bodyguard Bad Boys
Book 1: Rock Me
Book 2: Tempt Me
Novella: His To Protect

For the most recent Carly books, visit CARLY'S
BOOKLIST page
www.carlyphillips.com/CPBooklist

Carly's Originally Traditionally Published Books

Serendipity Series
Book 1: Serendipity
Book 2: Destiny
Book 3: Karma

Serendipity's Finest Series
Book 1: Perfect Fling
Book 2: Perfect Fit
Book 3: Perfect Together

Serendipity Novellas
Book 1: Fated
Book 2: Perfect Stranger

The Chandler Brothers
Book 1: The Bachelor
Book 2: The Playboy
Book 3: The Heartbreaker

Hot Zone
Book 1: Hot Stuff
Book 2: Hot Number
Book 3: Hot Item
Book 4: Hot Property

Costas Sisters
Book 1: Under the Boardwalk
Book 2: Summer of Love

Lucky Series
Book 1: Lucky Charm
Book 2: Lucky Break
Book 3: Lucky Streak

Bachelor Blogs
Book 1: Kiss Me if You Can
Book 2: Love Me If You Dare

Ty and Hunter
Book 1: Cross My Heart
Book 2: Sealed with a Kiss

Carly Classics (Unexpected Love)
Book 1: The Right Choice
Book 2: Perfect Partners
Book 3: Unexpected Chances
Book 4: Suddenly Love
Book 5: Worthy of Love

Carly Classics (The Simply Series)
Book 1: Simply Sinful
Book 2: Simply Scandalous
Book 3: Simply Sensual
Book 4: Body Heat
Book 5: Simply Sexy

For the most recent Carly books, visit CARLY'S
BOOKLIST page
www.carlyphillips.com/CPBooklist

Carly's Still Traditionally Published Books

Stand-Alone Books

Brazen

Secret Fantasy

Seduce Me

The Seduction

More Than Words Volume 7 – Compassion Can't
Wait

Naughty Under the Mistletoe

Grey's Anatomy 101 Essay

Grey's Anatomy 101 Essay

For the most recent Carly books, visit CARLY'S
BOOKLIST page

www.carlyphillips.com/CPBooklist

About the Author

NY Times, Wall Street Journal, and USA Today Bestseller, Carly Phillips is the queen of Alpha Heroes, at least according to The Harlequin Junkie Reviewer. Carly married her college sweetheart and lives in Purchase, NY along with her crazy dogs who are featured on her Facebook and Instagram pages. The author of over 75 romance novels, she has raised two incredible daughters and is now an empty nester. Carly's book, The Bachelor, was chosen by Kelly Ripa as her first romance club pick. Carly loves social media and interacting with her readers. Want to keep up with Carly? Sign up for her newsletter and receive TWO FREE books at www.carlyphillips.com.